WINCHESTER,

ACTUALLY

Stories by:

Maggie Farran

Catherine Griffin

Sally Howard

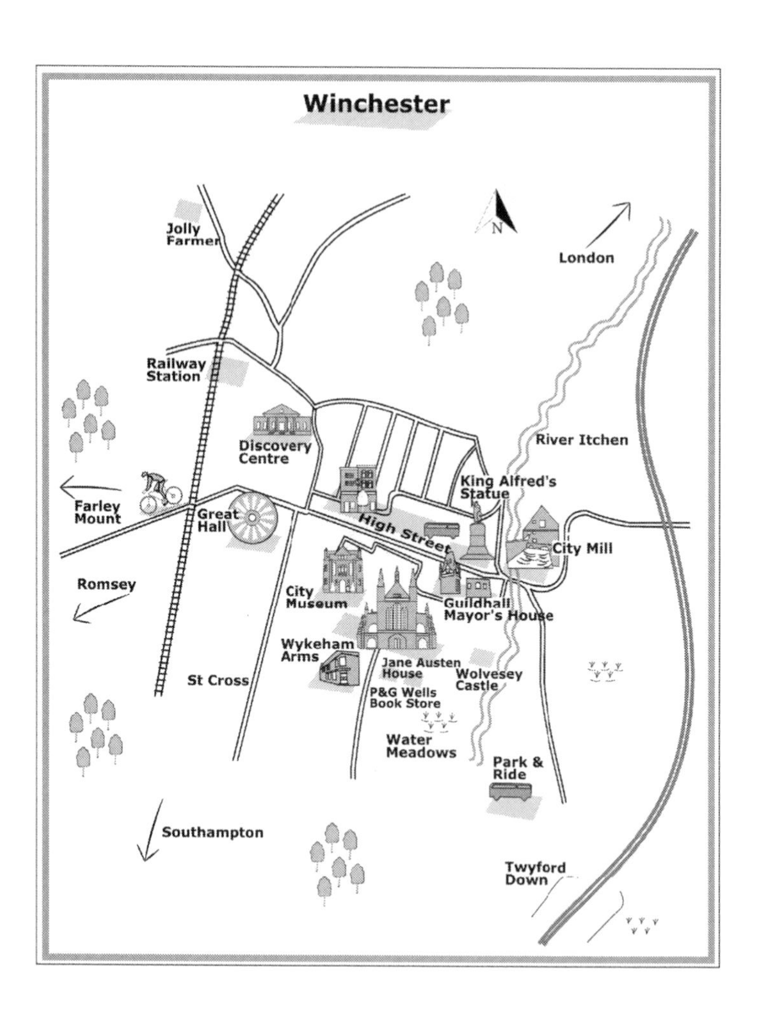
Winchester
N
Jolly Farmer
London
Railway Station
River Itchen
Discovery Centre
King Alfred's Statue
Farley Mount
Great Hall
High Street
City Mill
Romsey
City Museum
Guildhall
Mayor's House
Wykeham Arms
Jane Austen House
Wolvesey Castle
St Cross
P&G Wells Book Store
Water Meadows
Park & Ride
Southampton
Twyford Down

CONTENTS

The Tunnel, Part 1

Sally Howard

Settled continuously since pre-historic times, Winchester's history is never far from the surface, though you may have to dig a little.

'Wait!' Mark grabbed the hammer in Amy's hand. 'Slow down! If you knock that brick out, you'll bring the whole wall down!'

Amy glared at Mark and snatched the hammer back. Her shoulders ached with hefting the heavy black mallet and bashing it against the brick wall—the solid brick wall, which they had been going at for hours. She wiped her greasy hanky over her neck, sending up a fine cloud of dust from her ponytail. '*Why* are we even doing this?' she said.

She looked round the cellar of their cottage. Their picture-perfect, romantic cottage. Roses growing round the front door. Leaded glass windows. Perfect.

Mark said it was a very old cottage, with, apparently, some ancient history attached to it. It nestled in the leafy lane just down from the—also historically significant—ruined Manor House. When they'd bought the cottage, it was a dilapidated shell, but they had renovated and redecorated throughout. It had taken their money, but they had transformed it into their own lovely home. Their nest.

Except for the cellar, with its cold, damp chamber of red-brick walls. It was grim and claustrophobic. The dome-shaped ceiling was dotted with hooks—*what had gone on down here?*—she'd thought, as she had locked the heavy wooden door that led down from the kitchen, and placed a pretty chair in front of it. She'd tried her best to put the place out of her mind.

Now, Mark had suggested that they transform it into a modern den. With only modest structural re-engineering, the odd wall moved here and there, they could do it themselves, he'd said, his arms moving expansively. Enthusiasm had twinkled in his eyes like a kid building his first go-kart.

Which was odd really, because normally he was more interested in old and ancient things—which is why he'd found the cottage in the first place. With the cellar, he'd shown a new found enthusiasm for renovating. She guessed the attraction of a man cave was universal.

The wall in question, that they had been going at with hammers all morning, had appeared crumbly and insubstantial. It wasn't so much a wall, as a section of brick that jutted out into the room—like a chimney breast. Removing it would create more space, Mark had insisted. But the ancient mortar was solid as stone. Each smash of the hammer sent shock waves up her arms.

She dumped the hammer on the rubble-strewn floor and put her hands on her hips. That was it, no more. Time to get in the builders, do it properly. 'Why are we even trying to remove this wall anyway?' She scowled at him. 'I'm sure we could work round it.'

Mark shook his head. 'Amy, let's not rush. It's important to remove it.' He gave her an encouraging smile, turning back to the wall with his chisel.

She sighed and looked at the single red brick she'd been trying to work free with the hammer. It looked as though she'd loosened it. She lent down and gripped it with her fingers. The brick felt gritty and insubstantial. She pulled, crunching it from left to right. Suddenly it came away. She held it up triumphantly.

'See—look! I've done it—'

There was a rushing sound. The wall seemed to bulge outwards and then the whole thing collapsed in a roar like a storm at sea. She jumped back as bricks smashed to the floor. Dust clouds billowed like smoke. Grit shot up her nose and stung her eyes.

Gradually the noise died away. Mark emerged from a cloud of dust, his brown hair completely white like an old man. Incongruously he was grinning. He pointed to a small wooden door revealed in the wall behind.

'A door,' he observed.

'I can see that.' She scowled at him. Bricks were piled around her. They had missed crushing her feet by a matter of inches.

Mark wasn't worried about that—she saw enthusiasm blossom over his face. He was staring at the door. Old stuff, she realised.

'I'll get a torch.' He stepped past her. She heard him running up the stone steps to the kitchen.

She was left alone in the cellar. Avoiding looking at the door, she tidied away Mark's chisel and hammer and stacked them in the tool box. The electric light strung up on one of ceiling hooks left shadows in the corners—shifting, dust-filled shadows. She looked back at the door. It was strewn with cobwebs, hanging in gossamer sheets which floated in the air. It reminded her of the fake cobwebs that she'd bought at the supermarket for Halloween when the neighbours' kids came knocking.

The door itself was small—was it a door intended for people? Why was it bricked up? The idea of a door in her cellar, under her house, leading somewhere or letting in —

She heard Mark's footsteps clatter down the stone steps. 'I've got it,' he said, holding up a heavy-duty Maglite torch. He switched it on. It flickered. He gave it a thump on the side with the palm of his hand and it shone brightly. 'That's better,' he said, which reassured her not a bit.

There was a rusty bolt at the top of the door. Mark wrestled with it for a few moments before forcing it open in a shower of red rust. He pulled the door toward him. Age-old hinges scraped in protest. The door was open.

He shone his flickering torch into the inky blackness. 'Shall we?' he said.

Mark pulled back the curtain of cobwebs and stepped inside. Amy stepped forward, expecting to see a shallow storage room lined with shelves, or something like that anyway. Instead the light from Mark's torch bounced off brick walls. A narrow tunnel disappeared into darkness. She shivered.

Mark ducked his head through the door and started down the passageway, his torchlight flickering as he retreated into the dimness. Clearly the tunnel went in a long way—a narrow, cramped, dank tunnel. She had been stuck in a lift once. Only for an hour or so while they'd called the engineer. But it had been enough to leave her with a lingering sense of unease about small spaces.

Mark's voice echoed back to her. 'Aren't you coming in?' His torch appeared and then his face, grinning. He beckoned to her.

If she was going to go in she needed to do it now. She took a deep breath and stepped through the door. The bricked ceiling, the same old red brick from the cellar, was lower than she thought—she had to bend right over. It was cold and the air was stale. She thought of explorers of old entering Egyptian tombs, but altogether less glamorous.

She checked that the door behind them wouldn't swing closed, took a deep breath and followed him.

The tunnel curved round to the right. They shuffled along until the ceiling lifted and they could stand up straight. The light from the door disappeared behind them. It was stuffy, smelling like musty sheets. Her throat tightened. She thought again of those ancient explorers and the Egyptian curse—hadn't they died from breathing old stale air?

Mark stopped. She put her hand on his shoulder to look past him. His torch reflected a solid dirt wall in front of them. 'Is that it? Is it blocked?' she said.

'Yes. Darn-it, I thought it would go further.'

She moved in front of him so she could see his face. 'You *thought* it would go further?'

'It should go all the way to the old Manor.'

'Hang on a min—'

So that was it. Of course. He already knew about this tunnel. He'd been so keen on the cottage—so keen to redecorate. Now she realised why—to remove the stupid wall. To unearth a tunnel. To be the first to explore an ancient tunnel that had been buried for years, perhaps hundreds of years—what could be more up his street than that?

She stepped back, away from him. It wasn't so much his intent to find the tunnel that rankled with her. It was that he hadn't told her about it. Any of it.

Mark was standing there, flicking his torch up and down the bank of earth that blocked their way. The flickering made her eyes go funny. She reached to grab for the torch. 'Give me the torch, Mark.'

He handed it over to her. She angled the torch to light up his face. He wouldn't meet her eyes.

'You only chose our house because it had a tunnel?' She was trying to keep her voice level.

'It wasn't like that—'

'You wanted to knock down that wall. You knew what we'd find.'

He didn't respond. The tunnel felt oppressive. All the earth above her felt oppressive. Standing in a tunnel arguing with Mark felt oppressive.

Finally, he said, 'Well, yes, I was aware of some of the history.'

'I hate the cellar—you know that.'

He kicked at the earth with his feet. 'That's why I didn't say anything. Look, I'm sorry. I was going to investigate the tunnel first. Then we can board it up and re—' His voice trailed off. 'Hang on. What's that?' He clasped his hand over hers on the torch and swung it over the ground. Something flashed, catching the beam.

He stooped to pick it up. 'Look,' he said, his voice swelling with excitement. He held out his hand. A ring shone in the torch beam. Mark rubbed at the dull, grimy metal, bringing out the yellow gold beneath.

Amy picked it out of his hand. It was heavy, expensive. She angled it under the torch to get a closer look. 'There's an inscription on the inside.'

'It's posey ring. Given as a token of regard. Can you read the inscription?' Mark's voice was full of excitement.

Amy swivelled the ring in her fingers as she read: 'E - In God & thee my joy shall be - H.'

Mark looked up at Amy, eyes wide. 'This is fabulous. What a find! It must be her ring.'

'Her ring?'

'Her Ladyship's. Lord Henry and Lady Esther lived up at the old Manor.'

Amy raised her eyebrows.

'Apparently they were on the King's side in the Civil War. Lord Henry Wimborne went to London when war was declared. A message was sent to Lady Esther to warn her to escape.' Mark cleared his throat:

"A pair of fiery steeds did swiftly speed / to tell a message that she must heed. His Lordship's quest to divert the King / His foes did thwart and war did bring."

He cleared his throat again. 'Well, anyway. There's a whole rhyme about it.'

Amy gripped the ring in her fingers, wondering at its turbulent past. 'What happened to them?' she asked quietly.

'Her Ladyship was said to have fled down this secret passage from the Manor as the Roundheads were coming for her.' He shrugged his shoulders. 'I don't know whether she made it.'

A deep shiver ran over Amy. 'Poor lady. Do you think that the passage was blocked here and she didn't get through?'

Mark contemplated for a moment. 'Well, she must have got this far. After all, we just found her ring on this side of the blockage. The tunnel must have collapsed later.'

'She didn't make it any further?'

'I don't know.' Mark swung the torch back the way they had come and started off at a trot. 'C'mon. Let's have a look round the door.'

Amy had to race to catch up with him. She was relieved when she saw the light from the doorway. They crouched uncomfortably under the low ceiling.

Mark flashed the torch over the back of the door. It was black with age and mottled with cobwebs. She kept well back.

'So, let's assume she got this far,' said Mark, diving out of the door to fetch his chisel. He began gouging at the cobwebs. 'The bolt is on the other side. Someone would've had to let her out. The question is, did she get through the door? Or was she trapped in here? Or caught by the Roundheads.'

'How terrible…' Amy said faintly.

Mark glanced over his shoulder. 'You don't need to feel sorry for her, Amy. The aristos of that time were essentially overbearing overlords—'

'What? No. Why would you say that?'

''Cause of what is written down in history. It's not some romantic story like in your books….'

She glared at him, but he only shrugged. 'Reality is that the King's men were tyrants who would rather have seen thousands dead than relinquish any power. The King cut off his critics' ears when they didn't listen.'

She harrumphed. That sounded like something written by the King's enemies. 'But some were kind. Think of Downtown Abbey. They cared for their servants...'

'Honestly, Amy, that's a TV program. It would be naive to think that real life was like that.'

'And you just think it's all like Game of Thrones!'

But he'd turned away to the door that was being released from its shroud of webs. 'Aha!' he said, looking at her with glee written all over his face. He trained the torch in close to the wood around the edge. 'Scratch marks!'

Goose bumps raised on Amy's arms. She peered in. There were indeed scratches all around the door frame. Long scratches which showed a lighter brown than the rest of the wood. Sometimes single ones, sometimes five in a row. 'Those aren't ...?' she said, fearing the worst.

Mark stuck the torch under his chin, spooking his face. 'Someone t-trapped in here, t-trying to get out.'

That was the final straw. Her breath hitched in her throat. Her eyes darted to the looming tunnel behind them, where ghostly shadows swirled in the dust. Someone had been trapped here under her cottage. Lady Esther had run down the passage, fleeing for her life, only to end up so desperate that she had clawed at the door.

Amy flung herself out of the door, into the light and leant over, her hands on her knees.

Mark came up behind her. He placed a hand on her shoulder, lifting her up and rubbing her back. 'This has really got to you, hasn't it?'

She nodded, barely able to speak.

Mark slipped the ring onto her finger. It fit snugly on her third finger. The gold felt warm. She thought of the inscription, the delicate letters inscribed on the inside of the ring: *In God & thee my joy shall be*. It told of a husband who loved his wife. She wanted to believe that Lady Esther was a kind mistress. She wanted to believe, not the brief details that Mark had recounted, but that Lord Henry and his Lady were on the side of the just.

Most particularly, she wanted to believe that Lady Esther had escaped from her enemies and been reunited with her loving husband.

Mark was watching her with the ring. His expression was both soft and eager and then regretful as he cast a look at the door, 'We can have it boarded over, I suppose.'

They'd found a secret tunnel and some treasure—she couldn't deny him this adventure into the past. 'Ok, explore it if you want,' she said.

He nodded, closing his hand over hers. 'I'll try and find some more information. But don't go hero worshipping them. In all probability—'

She held up her hand. 'Stop. Don't tell me something horrible. I don't want to hear it. As far as I'm concerned, she got out, met her husband and he went on to be a great hero. That's what I'm going to believe anyway.'

He nodded, going over to shut the door.

She made him bolt it. Just in case.

Later that evening, Mark held the sheet of paper that he'd compiled with information about the fate of the two Royalists. Amy was right, he had found out about the house and its history before they'd bought the house.

He slid the paper into the shredder. Amy didn't need to know about the history, the real history, or at least what had survived from sparse accounts of the time. If she wanted to believe in the best, then so be it. And who knew, perhaps it wasn't the truth anyway?

The Tunnel, Part 2

Sally Howard

January 1642: King Charles feared for the safety of his family and fled London. Cities and towns declared their sympathies for the Parliamentarians or the Royalists. The majority of Hampshire was Parliamentarian, but Winchester became a Royalist stronghold. It soon came under siege from the Commander of the Parliamentarian army, who broke through the the city's walls forcing the Royalists in the Castle to surrender.

Subsequently, Parliamentary troops rioted through the city, pillaging and plundering as they went.

'Make haste, my Lady.'

She looked at the items on her dressing table. What to take—what to take? Her silver hair brush? The mirror? Too heavy—but their worth might be useful later. Some of her jewels were sewn into the hem of her dress—she would have enough money until she could meet up with Henry—no, she couldn't think of Henry now. Biting her lip, she picked up the silver hair brush and shoved it into her travelling bag.

'My Lady. They'll be here soon.' As Miss Bea spoke, loud banging reverberated through the house.

Esther snatched her woollen cloak from the bed and threw it over her shoulders. She hurried from the bed chamber and down the stairs. Miss Bea came clattering down behind her. Alexander, the butler, stood in the middle of the white-tiled hall. Grim-faced, he nodded as she ran into the kitchen.

The kitchen boy stood in front of the heavy wooden dresser. It had been pulled aside to reveal a doorway set in the stone wall.

'Hugh will show you the way. He's a good lad,' said Miss Bea, puffing up behind her.

Hugh's face brightened as she smiled at him, then crumpled at the sound of loud banging at the front door. They could hear shouting outside.

'Go,' said Miss Bea. 'We won't be able to hold them off much longer.'

'Take care, don't do anything brave.' She turned towards her elderly housekeeper, but she was pushing her through the door, closing it behind her. She heard the scrape of the bolt and a swoosh as the heavy drapes were pulled back. The wooden chest was pushed back into place.

She stared at the door, seeing nothing. The darkness was absolute, its weight pressing down on her and tightening her chest. She leaned towards the wall, feeling like a ship sinking below the dark surface of the sea—

'Are you all right, my lady?'

Hugh swung the lantern in front of her and her eyes adjusted to the tiny orange flame flickering inside.

'Yes, I'm all right. Shall we go?'

Holding the lantern high, Hugh led the way down a series of narrow steps. The passage flattened out. The sides were carved from dirt, roots sticking out like shrivelled fingers to brush her shoulders. The air tasted dank and stale and heavy in her mouth.

Hugh glanced back to check her progress. It was reassuring having him lead the way. Gradually the tight feeling in her chest subsided.

At one point she heard, or rather felt, the dull sound of thumping above them. Streams of soil flowed down from the roof like sand between fingers. The dust was gritty between her teeth.

'We're nearly there, milady. There'll be a horse ready.'

'Thank you,' she murmured.

The ceiling lowered and the passage narrowed further. The sides became brick rather than soil. She had to stoop and drag her bag along in the dirt. She wanted to ask how much further, but there was no point—she just had to keep going.

Hugh pulled up sharply. 'We're here,' he whispered. The lantern showed a small wooden door in front of them. 'It should be open.' He touched the wood and glanced back.

'Please go on.' Her voice sounded calmer than she felt.

The hinges creaked as he pushed the door. Suddenly it was flung open. Hugh yelped as he was pulled through from the other side, his lantern cracking to the floor

'Come out, Lady Wimborne,' said a man's voice.

She glanced at the black tunnel. Could she run? How far would she get? She was too late. Others had been sent to intercept her and they had arrived before her. All this—escaping down the tunnel, had been for naught!

She took a deep breath and stooped under the lintel of the door.

'Good evening, Lady Wimborne.'

She blinked, eyes adjusting to the light. In front of her, two grubby, round-headed helmets reflected a flickering torch stuck in a bracket on red-bricked walls. They appeared to be in some sort of cellar. The helmets belonged to two soldiers in leather jerkins who held swords pointed towards her—swords, which unlike their helmets, were clearly well maintained. Even if they held them casually and their pale faces were slack with boredom, she didn't doubt that they would use them ruthlessly. She recognised the Wray brothers—petty thieves and thugs for hire, the sort who did well in times like these.

Behind them stood a man that made a shiver run up her spine. Nathan Webb, self-styled captain of the county Parliamentary militia. A troublemaker who whipped up fear and mistrust amongst the populace. Everyone was at boiling point with the threat of war against their King. There were rumours of arrests, hangings in the Forest—

She swallowed heavily. A worse person she could not have hoped to meet.

And Hugh! They'd strung the boy up from the ceiling, snagging a hook into the back of his jacket—it was pulled tight under his armpits and he was spinning back and forth, kicking his legs frantically.

'I'm sorr—sorry, milady,' he stuttered. She stepped toward him. One of the soldiers moved into her path, pushing her down onto a wooden chair which stood in the centre of the room.

Nathan Webb had been watching her, leaning casually against the wall. 'Were you going somewhere tonight, Lady Wimborne?'

She stayed silent. Fear prickled up and down her spine.

He chuckled. 'You don't need to answer that of course,' he said, picking up her travelling bag. 'It's obvious that you are.'

He opened the bag and rifled through the contents. He held up her silver hair brush. 'Pretty. And valuable too.' He tossed it to one of the soldiers who grabbed it and shoved it down the front of his jerkin.

She squeezed her hands in her lap. The hairbrush had been her mother's.

The captain leaned down in front of her, smelling of sweat and damp clothes. 'Come, Lady Wimborne, we know that you're running off to meet your husband. My only question is, where are you going to meet him?'

She bit her lip and he smiled back at her. She realised that he was enjoying this—to extract the information too easily would be no fun at all for him.

Webb straightened up and looked around the cellar. His gaze settled on Hugh, who'd ceased his struggles and hung limply on his hook. Webb narrowed his eyes as he looked at the other hooks. Esther sat tensely on the chair, trying not to look at the soldiers who were leering at her.

The captain made a decision. 'Not that yet. After all you are a lady and I'm not *uncivilised* in my behaviour.' He turned towards the door to the passageway. 'Perhaps all that is required is some time for quiet reflection.'

He nodded to the soldiers and gestured to the door. He squeezed her arm as she passed. 'Lady Esther, you will tell me where your husband is. Everyone tells in the end. I am going to your house now and will return with whomsoever I find there. Being brave for yourself is commendable, but when someone else is involved...' He let the threat hang in the air.

One of the soldiers grabbed her under the arms and shoved her into the passageway. She stumbled, tipping forwards and clutching the packed earth of the floor to break her fall. The door slammed behind her. The last thing she heard was Hugh's cry of 'Milady.'

'Milady!'

Hugh kicked in the air as the door to the passageway slammed shut. His one small job was to escort Lady

Wimborne down the passageway and out to the horse which was tied up at the back of the cottage—and he had failed miserably.

In front of him stood the captain in the grey coat with the shiny buttons. The coat didn't fit properly—probably filched from someone shorter than himself. He was rifling through her travel bag. He was no gentleman, silver buttons or not.

He didn't like the look of the other two either. If he could get down from here, he would—he would—.

The captain flung her ladyship's bag at one of the brothers. 'Here, help yourself.'

The soldier caught the bag in his thick arms. The other still had her ladyship's silver mirror—Hugh could see it bulging at the front of his jerkin and his hands kept returning to it to check it was still there.

'You,' said the captain, 'Take this lad to the gaol in Cheriton. That should cool his loyalty. And you.' He pointed at the other soldier. 'Stay here and keep guard.' The captain turned on his heel and strode up the steps.

The soldier pulled a pearl necklace from the bag, but the other yanked the bag out of his brother's hands and upended it on the floor. A sly expression came over his face. He raised his eyebrows and cocked his head towards the steps out of the cellar.

The first brother frowned. 'You mean, what? Go? With these?'

'They're worth summat.'

'What 'bout the boy?'

'Take him with us.'

'He'll slow us down.'

'We'll deal with him, right? There's fresh horses. We'll be long gone, '

Hugh's heart beat wildly. What did they mean, deal with him? And, what about milady locked in the tunnel?

One soldier gathered up the lantern and bag, while the other grabbed Hugh round the legs and yanked him down from the hook. The back of his jerkin ripped, but he landed on his feet, ready to run. The soldier jabbed him in the ribs with his sword—not enough to hurt him or pierce his jerkin, but enough to make him move up the stone steps quickly, to the horses that were tied in the shadow of an oak tree. He was swung up into the saddle, the soldier clambering up behind him. He felt a sharp point beneath his ribs and dared not move as the soldier kicked his heels into the horse's sides. The horse started forward and a blast of rain-drenched wind caught him in the face. They rode off into the darkened night.

The bolt slid shut. Once again Esther was in darkness, this time with no lantern. Her heart beat loudly in her chest. She felt like she was shut in a tomb!

Calm down, she thought. What would it help to panic? Panic only freezes your mind and legs and chest and you won't be able to do anything with yourself...

She twisted her ring on her finger. The familiar warmth of the gold was soothing. The ring had been a gift from Henry. It had been engraved by the goldsmith on Jewry Street, the finest craftsman in the city. Henry was not normally given to shyness, but he'd lowered his eyes when he'd presented it to her. Her chest relaxed at the memory. Henry would want her to remain calm and think through the situation.

She realised it wasn't completely dark after all—a trickle of light shone round the edges of the door. Not enough to see anything with, but enough to take away the feeling that she was buried underground.

She pressed her ear to the wooden door. Faint voices were audible from the other side. They hadn't left yet.

She turned around. The tunnel loomed black and ominous. Could she feel her way along the passage? It was a terrifying thought. Even if she could hurry along it before Nathan Webb reached the house, then what? The door at the other end was locked shut and hidden behind drapes. Nathan Webb was no fool—he'd have left soldiers stationed at the other end. He had gone to fetch Miss Bea and Alexander, the butler. It was only a matter of time to bring them here and then what had he got planned?

She slid to the ground and pressed the palms of her hands into her eyes to calm herself.

Of course, she knew what they wanted—to find and arrest Henry. Henry had ridden to London to counsel the King. If the King would accept the Proposals which were being offered, perhaps, it would avert civil war.

She hoped that Henry had not shown his hand too early. His actions would openly declare himself a Royalist. That was a dangerous position to be in, outside of the protection of Winchester city walls.

Well, they could ask all they wanted: she didn't know where Henry was. He'd sent a letter earlier telling her to ride to Beaulieu and wait for instructions. She'd held the letter under the candlelight—a crumpled piece of paper with hastily scribbled words, barely discernible as Henry's writing. Henry had instructed her to burn and scatter the ashes—which seemed overly dramatic. Now she was glad of his foresight.

She shifted uncomfortably, the earth damp beneath her. It had been a few days since Henry had left—the letter the only communication to let her know that he was alive. Was he waiting for her at Beaulieu? Walking into a trap that would spring as soon as she led Nathan Webb's troops there?

She took several gulps of air while thinking what to do. Nathan Webb was a thoroughly unpleasant man, but harm and torture of the wives of powerful landowners would hardly be tolerated, even in these uncertain times. She would find a means to send a message to Henry about the rendezvous. Plenty of people in the surrounding countryside were secretly Royalists. They would help.

She felt better to have settled on a course of action and stood up. She was about to rap on the door when the light went out. The faint gleam that had been filtering round the edge of the door disappeared.

Her heart skipped a beat. What did it mean? Had they gone?

She pressed her ear to the door. Silence.

She rapped her knuckles on the wood and waited. Nothing. She rapped again and slammed the heel of her hand against the door. 'Help!' she shouted.

She felt with her fingertips round the edge of the door and pulled hard. It wouldn't budge. She scratched her fingers into any gaps. It was solid. Kneeling down, she searched blindly for anything that could be used as leverage, but there was only dirt.

She cradled her torn fingers under her arms. No one was there.

Some while later, she got up. She ran her sticky hands down her skirt. Something about the familiarity of the fabric calmed her. There was no point in letting her feelings overwhelm her.

She turned and felt with her hand for the side wall. She took a step forward. She knew the tunnel floor was flat—she only needed to keep stepping forward. She shuffled down the tunnel as it widened and the roof lifted. Relief flooded her when she could stand upright, even if the tunnel around her was still pitch black.

The floor inclined upwards and felt spongy underfoot. She didn't remember this part, when Hugh had led her down the passage earlier. How long ago that seemed.

The air was different—fresher. Her foot caught in earth and she stumbled. Steadying herself with a hand on the wall, she felt about with her toes. A pile of earth filled the tunnel. A patch of roof was lighter. Her heart beat faster—the tunnel had collapsed.

The pile of earth crumbled and slipped beneath her feet. She clawed at the soil with stiff fingers, pulling it down towards her and attempting to flatten and make it solid enough to stand on. A cool breeze flowed down from the hole, but it was too far out of reach. Jumping up, she could only just touch the rim.

Ahead of her the tunnel was blocked. She could go no further.

Feeling weak about the knees, she sank onto the pile of earth—and heard the crunch of hooves above her. A shower of soil rained down from the roof. It quickly became an avalanche. She covered her head with her hands. Clumps of soil bounced off her back, ran down her neck—

She strained to hear anything above the rush of rock and soil—

Dear Lord, was it Nathan Webb and his Parliamentarian troops returning? Would they find her here and drag her out of the tunnel? Was the tunnel collapsing?

'Essie,' came a harsh whisper.

'Henry!' She shoved her hand over her mouth to stop herself from crying out.

Henry's pale face appeared over the rim of the hole. Leaning over, he extended a hand and hoisted her up. Strong hands placed her on the ground. She was under a leafless oak tree, in the fresh night air.

Henry's arms were around her. She leaned against his chest. His coat smelt of smoke and cold air.

She looked up.

'I shouldn't have left you so long,' he whispered.

'You're here now—'

He set her apart and looked down at her. 'We must go. They've torched the house. They'll be here soon.'

Shock like sparks ran through her veins. Their home—gone. 'What about Miss Bea?'

'She got away.'

'And Hugh? What about Hugh? They took him—'

Henry touched his fingers to her lips. 'Don't worry, Essie. He's here.' He gestured to the back of the group—she saw two military men who she recognised as having ridden out with him, and behind them, Hugh, on a horse that looked far too big for him. He grinned at her.

'We ran into him and the Wray brothers. Nasty pieces of work but we were able to rescue Hugh and find out where you were.' He guided her to a horse, helping her up, before swinging up behind her.

'They're safe?' She turned to look at him over her shoulder.

'For the moment.' He held up his hand, signalling to move out. 'The king has rejected the proposals put to him—stupid blockhead that he is.' Henry's hands came round her waist and gripped the reins. 'We sought all means within our power. It was our last chance for peace.'

She felt cold. Henry ran his hands over hers, then stopped, feeling her finger. 'Where's your ring?'

Her ring—

She looked back. They were emerging from the trees, the hole to the tunnel left behind. 'I must have lost it in the tunnel.'

'Never mind, my love. I'll get you another. We must hasten.' He pulled the horse round to the east. The rolling hills that separated them from their city were cast in a dull flat silver by the full moon. The countryside looked peaceful—so normal—cradled between those familiar hills.

'Does it mean war, Henry?'

He squeezed her hand as he urged the horse forward. 'Yes. So help us God.'

Yesterday in College Street

Catherine Griffin

Jane Austen died 18th July, 1817, at 8 College Street, Winchester, where she had moved to be closer to her doctor, the surgeon Giles King Lyford. The brief notice of her death in the Hampshire Chronicle makes no mention of her being an author. During her lifetime, her books were attributed to 'A Lady'.

Deep in the novel she'd borrowed from the circulating library, Mary registered the sound of the front door closing, followed by her brother's heavy tread in the passage. She slammed the book shut, shoved it behind a chair cushion out of sight, and seized up her knitting moments before Giles ambled into the parlour.

As so often lately, it struck her how much Giles resembled their father. Though he looked well for a man of fifty, better than many men one saw about town. With his remaining hair pulled forward in the fashionable style, he had an amiable appearance, if not exactly handsome. Perhaps his middle had sagged but his shoulders were still unbowed.

No, he was hardly old yet. Why, he was only seven years older than her, and she wasn't an old woman.

'You're late from the hospital,' she said.

Giles lowered himself into his usual chair. 'A man was brought in, beaten about the head by a footpad. We did what we could for him, though he's not likely to live.'

Mary tutted. 'The hospital certainly get their money's worth from you. Up there all hours of the day and night. Then you have your other patients. You work too hard.'

'Oh, in another year or two, I'll hand it all to Henry. He'll be ready and I shan't grudge him, not a bit. No, I'll be happy smoking my pipe and growing roses, but I owe it to him to hand the business over in a good state, wouldn't you say?'

Mary smiled. It seemed only yesterday she'd been telling Henry off for playing with his top in the passage, and now he was twenty—a grown man.

She swapped her needles and started another row. 'I met Miss Barret in town today. Such a smart young woman, and so sweet-natured. I wonder she isn't married yet.'

'Uh-huh.' He picked up the newspaper.

Several weeks of diligent hinting had been without noticeable effect. The time had come for a more direct approach.

'Giles, do you ever think of marrying again?'

He looked up in surprise. 'What?'

'Marrying again. It's been two years, after all. No one would fault a man in your position for marrying, quite the contrary.'

'I rather think that's for me to decide.' He shook the folds out of the newspaper. 'I know you mean well, Mary, but I don't recall asking you to inspect every unmarried woman in Winchester. I don't plan to marry right now, and if I did, I'm quite capable of choosing my own wife.'

Taken aback, Mary lowered her knitting. She didn't want to fall out with him, and of course, she understood he might not want to marry again. His first wife's death had been hard enough, and then to lose his second wife—and so many babes too, over the years—but now she'd raised the subject, she could hardly drop it without deploying her most compelling argument.

'Well, I'm sure I don't wish to interfere where I'm not wanted. Indeed, if it were only yourself, brother, I would say nothing of it whatsoever. But there's more than your own happiness to consider. What of poor little Betsy? Misfortune enough to lose her mother at such a tender age, but is she to grow up in the charge of servants? I do what I can, but I'm only her aunt. Of course you miss dear Eliza, we all do. But for Betsy's sake, if not for your own, you really should exert yourself.'

She stopped for breath. Giles glared over his newspaper. Though he usually took her advice in good part, when annoyed he could have a very decided temper.

'Papa?' A tousled head of black curls peeked round the doorframe, shortly followed by two round brown eyes and chubby pink cheeks. 'Papa.'

Arms outstretched, the little girl ran to her father. The newspaper crumpled as he swept her into his lap.

'And how's my Betsy today? Behaving yourself for your aunt, I hope?'

The little girl beamed at him.

Mary held up her knitting. 'Your new jacket's nearly done, Betsy. Do you like it?'

'Pretty colour,' Giles said. 'The blue will suit her.'

'If you want, you may have stockings the same. Your old ones are more darn than anything.'

He chuckled and swung Betsy in the air before setting her feet on the floor. 'Go to your aunt now, child. Your father must work.'

'What? Going out again? You only just arrived.'

'I promised I would look in at College Street. It won't take long.'

'Oh.' Mary set her knitting on her lap. 'Of course, Miss Austen. How is she?'

To her, coming from a family of surgeons, the answer was clear on his face before he spoke. 'Comfortable enough, under the circumstances. I'll not be needed there many days more.'

'Oh dear. She's not old. Younger than me, isn't she?'

'Yes, I believe so.'

Since their father had been the Austen's family doctor and their cousin had married Reverend Austen's curate, Mary knew the family. She struggled to recall the girl Jane. A slight, talkative young thing, she thought, but perhaps she was confusing her with her sister.

'I must go.' Giles paused in the doorway. 'I shouldn't be long, but if not, don't wait dinner on my account.'

Mary nodded. She listened to his footsteps retreating down the passage. The front door clicked and clunked behind him. At her feet, Betsy had already tangled herself in blue yarn.

Mary patted her on the head. 'There's my good, clever girl. You did very well. Now—' She dug down the side of the chair and extracted her book. '—if you can be quiet, there should be just time to finish with Mr Darcy.'

Dust to Dust

Catherine Griffin

The London and South Western Railway completed the railway line connecting Southampton docks to Winchester, Basingstoke, and the London terminus, Nine Elms, in 1840.

Criminals were quick to seize the opportunities offered by the new transport links, and in 1851, Winchester was the scene of a significant, and still mysterious, theft from the railway. This fictional account was pieced together from newspaper reports of the crime.

Wednesday, 7th May 1851

It was pitch black inside the goods wagon. William Plampin sat in the corner, braced against the movement of the train. The sharp corner of a box dug into his calf, and with every passing minute, the train chuffed nearer to London and the end of the line.

He had to get out.

Getting in had been easy, just as Winter had said when he'd told William about the shipment.

'They load the wagons at the docks, right?' Winter had said. 'The doors are locked. A tarp is tied over the top.'

Winter knew what he was talking about. He was a porter at Nine Elms, foreman of the gang who unloaded the goods wagons. Winter was a clever young man full of bright ideas. Winter was going places. And he'd been right about the docks and the unguarded wagons.

William snorted. Disgusting, really, that people were such fools. Anyone could climb up and wriggle under the tarp, into the locked wagon.

Getting in *had* been easy. Getting out hadn't been. The opportunity hadn't come, and before he could escape the wagons were on their way to Southampton station.

'The train leaves Southampton around 9 at night,' Winter had said, 'reaches Nine Elms in the early hours. It may not be unloaded until next morning. The beauty of it is, they won't know where or when the boxes were taken. It's perfect.'

Right now, it didn't seem so perfect.

The train slowed, then stopped. William tensed. To find out where he was, he'd have to risk peeking outside. The train had stopped before, but only for a few minutes, and this might be another short delay. How long since Southampton? Perhaps an hour, though it seemed longer. Sitting in the dark, time stretched. If he had a chance to escape, he must be ready.

'It's too risky,' he'd told Winter.

'Risk? What risk? I'd do it myself in a shot if I wasn't working. Think about it. The stuff lies on the ground in California, free for anyone to pick up. You'll just be picking it up from a railway wagon instead. It's hardly even theft.'

The wagon lurched, moving again but slow. Could he jump from the train at this speed? That was one way out. But there were the boxes, those small, but very heavy boxes. His palms sweated at the thought of that weight.

'Gold.' Winter had whispered it. 'Gold dust. Think of it. One box, just one, would set us all up for life.'

He should have said no. He was too old to risk his life jumping in and out of trains. Gold, though... As Winter said, it was hardly theft. A box of gold was nothing to a wealthy banker, but William and his wife had no money, no children, no prospect but the workhouse in their old age. The gold would change their lives.

He should have known it wouldn't be so easy. But he hadn't, and now here he was, sitting in the dark on more money than he'd ever imagined. Trapped, as the train chugged on to the end of the line.

Again the wagon halted. Minutes passed in silence while William's heart thudded.

He stood, half-crouching with the tarp over his bent head, raised the edge, and peered out.

A quarter moon hung low over rooftops. The train had stopped in a siding, not a station. Drawing confidence from the quiet, he thrust his head out to look around.

All he saw were the four wagons from the docks, detached from the engine and the rest of the train. No one was in sight. The cool night air smelled of freedom. He filled his lungs, dizzy with the sudden inrush of hope.

What unbelievable luck.

Like any trapped rat, his first thought was to run, to be safe, but the gold held him as surely as if it were chained to his legs. He ducked back into the darkness of the wagon.

Each box weighed about 30lbs. He'd never imagined gold was so heavy. From his pocket, he took the bag he'd brought. The thin leather strained under the weight of one box. It wouldn't take another. He could carry another in his hand, though, and one under his arm. Three was the most he could manage.

He thrust his head out into the cool night air. All remained quiet. Train smoke mingled with the scent of damp grass, and under the grey moonlight, nothing moved. William pushed the bag out under the tarp and rested it on the covering of the next wagon, which sagged under the weight. He hooked his leg over the side of the wagon. For a moment he hung there, chest hard against the timber, clutching the boxes of gold. He wriggled over and fell, landing awkwardly on the coupling between the wagons.

He bit back a curse. Once he'd recovered his breath, he struggled upright and retrieved the bag.

In the distance a train chuffed softly. He sat on the coupling and lowered himself to the tracks. Gravel crunched underfoot.

He'd gone three steps before he noticed the passenger carriage hitched behind the gold wagon. Light flared in the dark window. William froze, hypnotised by the brief glimpse of face and hand illuminated by a match flame as the passenger lit his pipe.

The flame died. William lurched across the tracks into straggling bushes. Twigs clawed his face, branches snagged his clothes. He stumbled to a halt and crouched, hunched over the gold, shuddering and panting.

Then came the chug of an approaching train, matching his pounding pulse. Light swept over him. He pressed himself to the earth. He was small, he was covered by the bushes, he was dark as night. Invisible.

He dared not move. He hardly dared breathe. Still and silent as stone while the wagons rejoined the train and it chuffed away, heading for London.

The night's quiet flooded back. Cautiously, William sat up. The railway tracks glistened in the moonlight.

Elation flooded him. He was free. Free and alone in a strange town with three boxes of gold dust. No one knew the gold was missing, and they wouldn't, not for hours. No one should suspect him, but he couldn't afford to draw attention to himself.

He straightened his clothing and brushed off the worst of the mud. The bag concealed one box. He couldn't openly carry the other two. He slipped off his coat and ripped out the lining. It provided enough dark fabric to wrap the boxes.

But even covering the short distance from the wagon to the side of the tracks, he'd felt his arm was being wrenched from its socket. He had to face facts. Carrying three boxes would be a struggle. People would notice and wonder how such small packages could be so heavy.

A simple calculation: get away clean with two boxes or be caught with three.

He scraped a hole in the earth under the bushes, pushed one box into its shallow grave and covered it with dead leaves and dirt. Then he stood facing the tracks, fixing the place in his memory. The station must be down the track to his right. To his left, a road bridge arched over the railway line. The grass bank behind him sloped up to a fence.

He walked up the bank. Beyond the fence lay a grassy field and beyond that a large building with lights in the windows. He clambered over the fence and crossed the field to the road, where there was another fence to climb.

Now he just had to walk to the station and take the next train to London. At least the way led downhill. In the euphoria of escape, he'd forgotten how stiff he'd got sitting in the wagon, and his arm muscles already burned with the weight of the gold.

Someone was coming toward him, a broad, bow-legged man, eyeing him suspiciously from under his hat. William straightened his back and tried to walk naturally.

He gave the man a nod as they met. 'Good evening, sir. Do you know when the mail train leaves for London?'

The man squinted at him. 'Not 'til two.'

That was bad. William didn't want to hang around the station for hours. He needed a place to wait where he wouldn't stand out.

'Where can I get a drink?'

'The Eagle's not bad. Go down to the crossroads and it's on your left.'

William thanked him and strode on down the road, thinking only of the pub ahead and a sorely needed, well-deserved drink.

Friday 9th May, 1851

In the bushes beside the railway line, near the Andover Road bridge, a boy hunting for bird nests found something unexpected. Half-hidden under leaves and twigs lay a sturdy wooden box, about the size of a man's shoe.

Henry crouched to have a closer look. It was an interesting box, one that ought to hold something of value. He pulled it toward him.

Ten minutes later, Henry lugged the muddy box into the Jolly Farmer public house. He heaved it onto the bar counter.

From behind the bar, Jacob Keeling eyed the box and Henry sourly. 'What,' he said, 'is that?'

'Dunno. I found it,' Henry said. 'But I can't open it.'

'So why are you bothering me?' Jacob ran his fingers over the lettering on the side, then picked it up. 'God in heaven. Where did you get this?'

'By the railway line.'

'You know you oughtn't play down there,' Jacob said automatically. His mind was on the wooden box. It was well made, every joint tight, and the incised letters had an official look. What could be inside, to be so heavy?

Followed by Henry, he carried the box into the kitchen.

His wife Elizabeth greeted their arrival with raised eyebrows. 'What trouble are you in now, Henry Turpen?'

'The boy found this box by the railway line.' Jacob handed it to her. 'What do you think?'

'He's not meant to go down there—' Her eyes widened as she felt the weight. 'This was by the railway?'

'Aye, just by here,' Henry said.

'Whatever it is, it's not ours,' she said. 'Maybe it fell from a train. We'd best take it to the station.'

As usual, Eliza had the right answer.

Having seen her and Henry off to the station, Jacob returned to the bar. A customer was waiting to be served, a London man by his accent, middle-aged, pale and unhealthy looking. He paid for one beer and nursed it for over an hour, watching the road through the window.

By the time Eliza returned the pub had filled with thirsty locals, and they were both too busy to notice when the stranger left.

William Plampin walked from the Jolly Farmer down to the bridge, where he stopped to look down at the railway tracks. Low sun painted the western sky pink but full darkness lay hours away. There were still too many people about.

When he'd reached London, he'd left the gold with Winter, who said he had a buyer lined up. Of course, they'd not get the full value, and Winter would take his share, so it wouldn't be a fortune. Still, William was much richer than he had been.

But he couldn't forget the box he'd left behind, just yards from where he stood now, hidden under that bush. He hadn't told Winter about the third box.

Collecting it was a risk, though a small one. The police were bumbling about Nine Elms, questioning everyone to no purpose. They hadn't a clue yet, probably never would.

He tore his gaze from the bushes. For now, he had to wait. With or without the gold, he'd return to London on the mail train, so he had plenty of time to make his mind up.

William ambled down the Andover Road to the crossroads, a much shorter journey than he remembered. He passed the Eagle Tavern, went down the lane and into another street, and turned left there, intending to walk a circuit. He stopped outside the White Swan Inn. The smell of roasted meat gripped his stomach and tugged him through the door, into the warm fug of smoke and laughing, talking men.

He took a corner seat and ordered a plate of chops. Alone and ignored among the crowd of cheerful locals, he relaxed, or tried to. The hidden gold burned in his brain.

It couldn't be too hard to find a buyer. It was *gold*. He could tuck the box under his bed for a year or more, sell it little by little not to attract suspicion. No need to split the money with Winter. It would be William's bonus, his and Mary's. Why not, when he was taking all the risk?

His food came, but his hunger had fled. The meat he forced down landed in his gut as a cold dead weight. As the grease congealed on his uneaten chops, he reached a decision.

He still had time to kill, so he had a drink to steady his nerves, and then a few more. By the time he headed back to the Andover Road, his nerves were so steady he was positively cheerful.

Night had fallen and few people were about. He reached the Andover Road bridge, surprised to find himself there so quickly.

In the faint cloud-reflected moonlight, the tracks went their serene way, marking a straight true line across the world. A line from here to there, past to future, cutting time and distance at a stroke. What a wonderful thing was the railway.

No one was in sight. He crossed the bridge and climbed the fence into the pasture. The lights of the Jolly Farmer pub glowed warm and welcoming from the night. He turned his back on them and followed the fence to where it bordered the railway embankment. He climbed over and scrambled down to the tracks, the rough turf catching his feet in the darkness. He pushed his way into the straggling bushes. It was too dark to see where the box was hidden. He knelt and began to feel around. His hands found only dirt and twigs and damp leaves. No box.

Frantically he rifled through the leaf litter. The box must be there, he must just be missing it somehow. Had he buried it deeper than he thought? Maybe his memory had tricked him, and the box was nearer the track, or more to the left…

A heavy hand fell on his shoulder. 'You're under arrest.'

William leaped to his feet. He peered up at the young man's triumphant grin. 'What for? I ain't done nothing wrong.'

'Trespass on railway property, for starters. Come on.'

As William was marched toward the station, unease stirred the warm fog of alcohol. The young man had a local accent. He wasn't a police detective. Had he been lying in wait? Had the box been found?

But even if they'd found the box, they couldn't have any evidence linking him to the robbery. It was all circumstantial. He might have been wandering the railway line for some entirely innocent purpose, though he couldn't think of one right now.

The London train stood in the station, and three men beside it on the platform: the station master, a police sergeant, and the third, not in uniform, looked like a police detective.

William stiffened. Too late to run now, even if he could. He shrank into his coat.

The three men turned at their approach.

'What do you have there, Mr Gradidge?' the station master asked.

'I caught him, Mr Dean!'

'So I see. Caught him doing what?'

Gradidge expanded with pride. 'I kept watch on the spot where the boy found the gold, and sure enough, this man came looking for it. He's your thief!'

'That was most enterprising of you, Mr Gradige. Well done.' The station master turned to the detective. 'Mr Field, it seems we've done your job for you.'

Field smiled wryly. 'One mustn't jump to conclusions in this business. What's your name, fellow?'

'William Plampin,' William said. 'And I'm no thief.'

'Your business?'

'Tailor.'

'Show me your hands.'

William held out his hands palm up, trembling slightly. The detective had cold intelligent eyes that reminded him of Winter, and he didn't like it.

Field peered at his hands. 'I don't think you've done much sewing lately. See any needle marks, Shaw?'

The sergeant grunted.

'Work's been slow,' William said. 'That's why I'm here, looking for work.'

'On the railway line at midnight?'

William had nothing to say. He kept his silence as Gradidge handed him into the sergeant's custody.

It was pure dumb luck of the worst sort. He'd been in the wrong place at the wrong time, but they couldn't prove he'd ever had the gold in his hands. They wouldn't find gold in his house. He'd left it with Winter. And Winter, the sly bastard, would have sense enough not to be caught with it.

And there was the rub: Winter had all the gold, but for a big theft like this, the police would have to catch someone. Someone had to take the blame and the punishment, and that was poor unlucky William Plampin.

There really was no justice in the world.

HISTORICAL NOTES

This story is based on reports of the theft in the Hampshire Chronicle, Times, and other records, though to reconstruct the events I had to use some imagination. In particular, how exactly the theft was carried out—and by who—remains unknown, though witnesses reported William Plampin in Winchester that night, carrying a bag and departing by the mail train to London.

Plampin was found guilty of receiving stolen goods and sentenced to ten years transportation.

William Winter, a porter at Nine Elms station, absconded, leaving behind his wife. I found no further record of him or the stolen gold.

Plampin and his wife Mary later testified against Winter and others involved in an unrelated, earlier theft from the railway. In this case, Winter was the thief and Plampin fenced the goods.

While in Winchester prison, awaiting transportation, Plampin petitioned for release on grounds of ill-health. One of the letters supporting his petition was written by members of the board of the London and South-Western Railway. He had apparently convinced them he was not involved in the gold theft after all. It seems the petition was successful, as a William Plampin is recorded as having died in London in 1860 (he would have been about 47), and Mary Plampin appears in the 1861 census as a widow.

Detective Charles Field is mentioned in "The Suspicions of Mr Whicher" by Kate Summerscale.

Raising Alfred

Catherine Griffin

The large bronze statue of King Alfred the Great is one of Winchester's most famous landmarks. Commissioned by the City to mark the millennium of Alfred's death, it was erected in 1901.

10th September 1901

A sea of hats filled the Broadway. Men and women crowded against the temporary fencing, small children perched on shoulders and schoolboys crouched to peek through knotholes. All were eager for the slightest glimpse of the new statue. Grey overcast with a hint of drizzle hadn't dampened the cheerful buzz of expectation.

Here to see history, Driscoll thought. *Or at least a good show.*

A glance at his pocket watch confirmed it was past four in the afternoon. If the morning had gone to plan, the statue would have been up hours ago. As it was, they'd be pushed to finish today.

Even with his back to the crowd, he felt their eyes on him, like an itch between his shoulder blades. And then there was his other audience...

Thornycroft, the sculptor, stood watching the workmen round the statue. He was a tall man, broad shoulders only slightly stooped with age. His cane tapped the ground in a nervous tattoo.

Doesn't trust us to lift his precious statue without watching our every move.

Thornycroft turned, as if sensing the inspection, and paced toward him. *Tap, tap, tap,* went the cane.

'Will we be lifting soon?' he asked.

Driscoll eyed him coldly. 'When we're ready, sir.'

Thornycroft rocked on his heels. 'Are you a father, Driscoll?'

'I don't have that pleasure yet.'

'My fourth entered the world last week.' Thornycroft glanced at him, smiling. 'This is nearly as nerve-wracking.'

Ignoring the sculptor, Driscoll focussed on the statue: King Alfred with sword upraised, modelled in five tons of bronze, seventeen feet tall, intended to stand on a twenty-foot block of Cornish granite. Wrapped in green fabric and stout coils of rope, the figure stood with its back to the stone block. Over it the shear legs, an A-frame of stout poles, pointed to the grey September sky. Taut guy ropes ran from the poles to trees along the Broadway. The traction engine chuffed gently and the workmen waited, ready with timbers to shore up the statue as it rose and ropes to guide its final placement.

Once more Driscoll eyed the timbers and the ropes, mentally reviewing each knot, each step in the process. Everything had been checked and re-checked. Still, there remained a nagging doubt.

But the men knew their work, and so did he. They'd lifted heavier loads. The buzz of the crowd and Thornycroft's tapping was playing on his nerves, that was all. After all the preparation, all the checks, all the care and thought in the world, one had to have faith that ropes and timber and men would do their jobs.

'You may want to stand back, sir,' he said.

Thornycroft shuffled back to the fence.

Driscoll caught the foreman's eye. 'All ready?'

'Aye, sir.'

'Let's get to it then. Start the engine.'

The foreman waved to the waiting engine man, who turned a wheel. The engine chugged. Slowly, steadily, it hauled in the slack rope. The shear legs shivered as the ropes pulled tight. Timber and rope creaked, and the crowd murmured. Steam and smoke puffed from the engine with the sharp smell of burning coal and hot oil.

Driscoll clenched sweating hands. He felt the rising strain in his own shoulders, as if it was himself racked between the remorseless engine and five tons of bronze.

The statue stirred.

Driscoll held his breath. 'Be ready to shore it up.'

The workmen nodded, not taking their eyes from the statue.

Something cracked like a pistol shot.

Everyone froze. To gasps from the watching crowd, the poles swayed. Wide-eyed workmen stumbled back, dropping the timbers.

'Shut off the engine.' Driscoll strode toward the statue, shouldering a man aside. 'Get those timbers in.'

The left-hand pole of the shear legs snapped. Screams and shouts rose from the crowd. The statue thumped to earth. Workmen scrambled past Driscoll, shielding their heads from falling ropes and pulleys and splintering poles. One of the heavy timbers glanced off the upraised arm of the statue.

A sharp pain hit Driscoll's head. His legs were suddenly rubbery, unable to hold him up, and the ground rushed to meet him.

'Driscoll? Driscoll, can you hear me?' The voice rang clear then receded like waves on a shingle beach. 'Hold his head up.'

'Give him some air.'

'His head's bleeding...'

'I told him shear legs was no use. Shoulda used a tripod...'

'Don't be daft, man. It was the guy rope broke. They were damp. It was the damp done it.'

Driscoll opened his eyes. Thornycroft's face swam into focus: pale, hatless, grey hair wild.

'He's awake! Driscoll, are you all right?'

'Ugh. What happened?' Driscoll tried to sit. Multiple hands helped him. He fought off a wave of dizziness.

'A rope broke,' Thornycroft said. 'But don't worry about it now. The police ambulance is coming.'

'I'm all right.' Driscoll lifted a hand to his head. His fingers touched warm, sticky liquid. He winced at the sharp sting. 'What's the damage? Anyone injured?'

'No, no. Only you. Do stay still. You may be more badly hurt than you realise.'

The circle of concerned faces round him blocked his view of the statue. He remembered the shear legs breaking, the sickening crack of timber. If the statue was damaged… The celebrations were scheduled for the 18th, complete with speeches and marching bands, pageants and choirs. The statue had to be ready for unveiling. His stomach twisted.

'The ambulance is here,' Thornycroft said. 'Can you stand?'

'I don't need an ambulance.'

Thornycroft helped him up. His head swam. The world turned starkly black and white like a photograph and the sea roared in his ears. A policeman steered him toward the waiting stretcher.

Driscoll twisted, trying to see the damage. 'I can't go. There's work to do.'

'Don't worry about that now,' Thornycroft said.

Through the shifting crowd of men, Driscoll glimpsed the shattered shear legs, splintered into matchwood, tangled in ropes and pulleys. One fact was certain; they wouldn't be raising the statue today.

Firm hands strapped him to the stretcher. He had no energy left to protest.

It was a long walk from the hospital, down the hill to the High Street and back to the Broadway. When he saw the statue ahead, Driscoll paused to recover his breath.

Most of the on-lookers had dispersed. Despite the late hour, his men remained on site though they didn't appear to be working.

Lazy devils, he thought. *Any excuse to be idle.* He strode toward the statue. One man noticed his approach and they all streamed out to greet him, raising a ragged cheer.

'I'm fine, I'm fine.' Shrugging off their questions, he walked on through the gate in the fence around the site.

To his surprise, Thornycroft was waiting for him. 'Good God, man, what are you doing here? You should be in hospital.'

'Nothing worse than bruises.'

'Even so...' Thornycroft shook himself. 'That was a close shave. You could have been killed.'

Driscoll looked around. The workmen had tidied the wreckage, at least. There wasn't much else they could do tonight. He nodded to the foreman. 'Carter, have the men pack up and send them home.'

'Right you are, sir.'

The statue remained, swathed in green fabric, standing beside the granite block. Driscoll leaned on the scaffolding. 'Any damage?'

'Not a scratch,' Thornycroft said. 'I must confess, I checked him first—had the shock of my life when I realised you were hurt. I'm heartily relieved to see you on your feet.'

Driscoll took a deep breath. His head ached dully but the dizziness had passed, leaving only an odd sense of distance from himself. But Alfred was all right, and that was the main thing. He climbed the scaffolding onto the rough granite block where Alfred would stand. Thornycroft followed him, and they sat side by side, gazing up the High Street.

'He'll have a good view,' the sculptor said.

It was a good view: the High Street stretching before him, and to his left, the park and the Guildhall. Strange, Driscoll thought, how different things looked from here. Perspective, he supposed. Strange too, to think that Alfred would enjoy this view for the next hundred years or more.

'A guy rope snapped,' Driscoll said. 'And the shear legs couldn't take the strain. The pole broke. Maybe the ropes were damp. We rigged them to the trees last night. I should have thought—'

'Accidents happen.' Thornycroft sighed. 'Don't blame yourself. Lucky, really, it happened when it did. If he'd dropped farther, it could have been a lot worse.'

Below them, the workmen chatted as they collected their tools ready to leave for the day. Muted music drifted from a nearby public house.

'This matters to us,' Driscoll said. 'In a hundred years, people will look up at this statue and they'll remember you. Not me, or Carter, or the man with the traction engine, but we're part of it, all the same. Part of history.' He stopped, feeling awkward. He didn't normally say such things.

'I know what you mean. In truth, I doubt they'll remember me either, but if Alfred is here, that's enough for me.'

'Your youngest child,' Driscoll asked. 'Boy or girl?'

Thornycroft shifted in his seat. 'Girl. If it was a boy, he would have been named Alfred. What do you think of Elfrida?'

Driscoll suppressed a grin. 'Very nice. As for our Alfred, we'll order in stronger ropes and timbers. We'll have it done in time.'

'I'll hold you to that.' Thornycroft clambered onto the scaffolding. 'And when he's up, I'll stand you all dinner.'

While the sculptor descended, Driscoll stood for a last look up the High Street.

Yes, he thought. *He'll have a pretty good view.*

HISTORICAL NOTES

This story is based on real events: the first attempt to raise Alfred failed when the lifting gear broke. The contractor, Driscoll, was taken to hospital, but walked back to the site later that day.

The sculptor Thornycroft was present. His daughter Elfrida was born on the 5th September, just 5 days before.

After the statue was successfully raised on Saturday 14th September, Thornycroft treated the workmen to dinner, including champagne.

If you are interested, the Hantsphere online collection has photographs of the main stages of work on the statue.

At King Alfred's Statue

Maggie Farran

Despite the traffic, King Alfred's statue is still a good place to arrange to meet a friend, or someone you'd like to know better.

Where was James? He was always so punctual. Eva had been waiting for fifteen minutes now and it was getting chilly. She did up the brass buttons on her wool jacket. She had chosen the jacket carefully as it was a cheerful cherry red and went well with her skinny black jeans. She brushed her dark curly hair away from her forehead in a brisk motion.

She always met James at the huge imposing statue of King Alfred at the bottom of the High Street. It suited them both as they walked there from opposite directions. Eva lived up St Giles Hill in a little Victorian terrace. James lived in a modern flat in Hyde near the station.

They had only been going out for a few weeks and they enjoyed each other's company. At least she enjoyed his company and she hoped it was reciprocal. He was kind and funny. He made her feel good about herself. He was always giving her little compliments about how young she looked for her age, how smart she looked and how interesting he found her. They had met through the Guardian personal column.

'Widower in his early fifties seeks companionship. Enjoys going to the theatre, concerts and reading. Lives in Winchester.'

Eva had never answered an advert like this before, but it was three years now since Brian had died. She was busy enough with her choir and art classes, but she missed male company. She wanted someone to go to the theatre with, who wasn't a female friend. James was exactly what she had wanted.

She still missed Brian terribly. They had been married for almost thirty years. They had married in their early twenties and grown up together. He had been quiet and reliable. He hadn't been romantic but she had always felt loved and secure.

She rang James's mobile but there was no answer. Perhaps he had had second thoughts, but he had given her no indication last time they met that he wanted their friendship to end. He was so polite and considerate that it was so out of character for him not to let her know if he couldn't make it. She waited another ten minutes and then rang his mobile again. Still there was no answer.

She had never been inside his flat although she had had a little look outside when she'd known he wouldn't be there. So far, they had met on neutral ground. They had been to the Everyman cinema to see a live screening of Hamlet, sitting awkwardly on the double sofa seat trying not to spill their cups of coffee and being mutually irritated by the young couple beside them, noisily tucking into a huge pizza. They had also had a meal together at Alfie's pub. They had sat outside, and the evening had gone well. She had felt relaxed in his company and she hoped James had too. That had been their last meeting and she went over their conversation in her mind. She couldn't think of any indication that he wasn't as happy as she was.

She looked at her watch again. He was half an hour late now.

She walked up the High Street and turned right down Jewry Street. She walked past the Discovery Centre and the Theatre Royal and then crossed onto Hyde Street. His flat was in a side street called Silchester Rise.

She had been walking at a brisk pace but now she slowed down. She didn't know quite what to do. Would he be annoyed that she had turned up or would she find that he was ill in bed and had turned off his mobile? She looked up at his flat and there was a light on. She plucked up her courage and rang his number on the intercom.

A woman answered. 'Hello?'

'Hi, is James there?'

'Sorry there's no one called James in this flat. I'm Barbara. I don't know any James.'

'Sorry. I must have made a mistake.'

Eva shivered. She was certain this was the address James had given her. He must have been lying. She couldn't believe it. Why would he have lied to her? He had seemed so honest and straightforward. She had always prided herself on being a good judge of character.

She retraced her steps and found herself back at her little cottage. She poured herself a large glass of red wine and plonked herself down on her sofa. She reached forward for the remote and switched on the television. She shuffled her way through various channels and settled on a programme about the National Trust hosted by Alan Titchmarsh. She couldn't concentrate on it, but she found his voice strangely reassuring. He really was honest and trustworthy. He wouldn't pretend to live somewhere that he didn't. She poured herself a second glass of wine and just as she was about to take her first sip her mobile rang. It was James. She was tempted to ignore it, but her curiosity got the better of her.

'Hi Eva, I'm so sorry. I had an emergency. My mother had a mini stroke and I had to take her to hospital. In all the panic I left my phone in my flat. I can't apologise enough.'

'How is she now?

'Oh! She recovered very quickly, but she's got to stay in overnight and have a few tests done in the morning.'

'Would you like me to come over to your flat and keep you company?'

There was a long pause. Eva held her breath and waited, interested to hear how he would wriggle out of her suggestion.

'That's so kind, Eva, but to be honest I'm exhausted. I'll give you an update in the morning.'

Eva sipped her wine and went over the conversation. She didn't know what to believe now. He must care about her a bit otherwise he wouldn't have bothered to phone and apologise. He had sounded so sweet and genuine. There must be some explanation for him lying about the flat or perhaps she had been mistaken about the number or rang the wrong bell.

The next morning after a sleepless night Eva forced herself out of bed. After her shower she felt better and went downstairs to her cosy kitchen at the back of the house. It looked out on her tiny garden. It was full of tulips at the moment standing tall in a multitude of colours. She got so much pleasure from her garden. She watched the birds feeding from her bird table. She began to feel calmer and made herself a bowl of porridge in the microwave.

She had just eaten one spoonful when her mobile rang. She didn't answer it. She was going to eat her porridge in peace, she decided. Ten minutes later it rang again and she answered it.

'Hello, James, how is your mother doing?'

'Oh! She's doing fine. I'm picking her up from hospital now. I'm going to stay with her for a few days until she feels happy to be left on her own.'

'Would you like me to do some shopping for her? Where does she live?'

'Oh no that's very kind of you, Eva, but I've got that all under control. Shall we meet up tomorrow evening in the usual place at seven o'clock? We could have something to eat and I'll tell you how she's getting on.'

Eva found herself agreeing to the meeting despite her uneasiness. James sounded his usual kind and thoughtful self. There must be some explanation to the mystery of his address.

James was already waiting for her when she got to King Alfred's statue. He smiled and gave her a hug.

Eva stiffened. She felt suspicious now and wanted a few more explanations.

'How is your mother, James?'

'She's doing fine now. It was just a mini stroke. There's no lasting damage. It's just been very frightening for her. That's why I'm going to stay with her for a bit until she's got her confidence back.'

'Where does she live? Perhaps I could have some flowers delivered.'

'Oh no, there's no need to do that. It's a very kind idea but she's a private kind of woman. She wouldn't want any fuss. I thought we could go for a walk along by the river and then have something to eat, if that's ok with you?'

It was a warm evening for May and Eva found herself relaxing and enjoying the walk. She and James always had plenty to say to each other. The River Itchen was very attractive with the water meadows and views up to Saint Catherine's Hill. A lone swan swam by and they stopped to watch it.

'I wonder where his mate is,' she said. 'Swans are supposed to be faithful to their mate for their whole life. I don't know if that's true or not.'

'Well, it's a lovely idea, but I doubt it's true.'

They retraced their steps and had a meal at The Bishop on the Bridge. It was just about warm enough to sit outside with their coats on. They enjoyed the view of the river and the old bridge. The food was delicious and after a glass or two of wine Eva felt her trust in James returning. She must have made a mistake about the number of the flat, she decided.

'I'll walk you back to your house.'

'Thank you, James, that's kind of you.'

Eva had agreed readily enough, but as soon as they got to her front door, she wished she hadn't. She wasn't ready to ask him in yet. That seemed like a big step for her.

'Aren't you going to ask me in for a coffee?' James said gently.

Eva felt very awkward refusing him. He kissed her on the cheek and said kindly, 'No rush, Eva, I understand. Shall we meet up on Friday at seven?'

Eva agreed, relieved that he still wanted to see her. She made herself a hot chocolate and tried to watch the television, but she just couldn't concentrate. She really liked James. He was an interesting, intelligent man. She so wanted to trust him but there was something about him that made her feel uneasy. She decided to google him. She put in his name 'James Vincent' and then added 'Winchester'. Nothing came up that was anything to do with him, but then that wasn't all that odd, she thought, for someone of his age.

She was shopping in town the next day when quite by chance she caught a glimpse of James in Marks and Spencer's café. He was talking intently to a smart-looking woman, and sitting next to her was a little girl who looked about six. Eva hid herself as best she could and pretended to look at the bright summer dresses hanging on the rail next to her.

After ten minutes James got up followed by the woman and child and walked down the stairs into the High Street. Eva followed them keeping at a safe distance just as if she were in some detective drama. They walked quite slowly with James holding the little girl's hand. She skipped along beside him. They turned right into the Abbey Gardens and the little girl ran off toward the playground.

'Push me, Daddy,' she shouted.

James ran to her and started to push her on the swing.

Eva sat down on a bench some distance away. She started to shake. She couldn't believe what she had just heard. James had never mentioned any children. She had given him plenty of opportunity when she had told him all about her son, William, in Australia. She had told him how she visited every other year and how much she missed him. He'd been very understanding. In fact, she could distinctly remember him saying how sad he and his wife had been that they were unable to have children. She'd felt sorry for him and his poor dead wife.

She watched from a distance as James and his daughter played happily together in the park. The woman was busy looking at her phone when the little girl called, 'Mummy, look what I've found.' The woman looked over and joined her daughter. Eva couldn't hear what they were saying but they seemed to her to be a happy little family enjoying time together.

On Friday Eva thought about her meeting with James and was determined to go through with it. She was curious to find out what lies he would tell and how he would wriggle out of it.

He greeted her at King Alfred's statue with his usual charming smile. She had taken trouble with her outfit and felt attractive in her new cheerful yellow summer dress.

They chatted away together until Eva said: 'I saw you in the Abbey Gardens yesterday pushing a little girl.'

James didn't miss a beat, 'Oh yes, that was my niece, Sophie. She's my younger sister's little girl. Sweet little thing.'

'Funny that she called you Daddy. I'm afraid you've burnt the cakes this time. I can't stand liars. I can't believe you strung me along for so long. Goodbye, James. I hope I never have the misfortune to meet you again.' Eva strode off with her head held high.

She walked and walked until she found herself wandering along by the River Itchen. The water was clear and bright. The lone swan stretched its elegant neck as it swam past her followed by three tiny cygnets. Eva stopped and took a deep breath. She had decided she was going to ring her son, William, and book flights for a holiday in Australia. She felt a new strength. She would be alright on her own, she felt sure.

The Gun Riot

Catherine Griffin

King Alfred's statue was raised in 1901 with great civic pride, and that pride was again evident in 1908, when an extravagant historical pageant was planned to raise money for repairs to the cathedral. But not everyone was happy: working men were discontented with inflation and stagnating wages.

Monday 25th May 1908

It was Empire Day, and the first day of Constable Pike's police career saw him patrolling Winchester High Street. Or at least, Head Constable Felton was patrolling; Pike just plodded.

Felton had mastered a special walk: steady, deliberate, relaxed. Not the stride of a man with a destination in mind, but not an idle stroll or saunter. It was the walk of a man with all the time in the world to look, and see, and be seen.

Pike's lanky legs, encased in stiff new uniform trousers, didn't have the knack. He shuffled a pace behind Felton, trying not to gawk at the shop windows and smartly dressed townsfolk like the country boy he was.

Meanwhile, Felton nodded to one passer-by after another. 'Good morning, sir. Lovely day. Morning, ma'am. How's the wife, John?' Most smiled and nodded, or tipped their hats in return.

Reflected in a haberdasher's window, Pike glimpsed himself as a blue-uniformed stranger with the expression of a stunned bull calf. He looked every bit as stupid as he felt.

He'd only joined the police because he was tall and it was steady work and had to be better than mucking out cows in the winter. Boyishly, he'd imagined himself arresting burglars and chasing footpads through midnight streets, but so far, reality was a tight scratchy collar and a lot of standing around. He was starting to wish a crime would happen—not murder, of course, maybe a theft—just to relieve the boredom.

Behind him, a horse clip-clopped down the street. Pike turned to see Felton watching a pony and trap.

Posters covered the sides of the trap, each declaring in large block letters: Protest Meeting Today 7.30 pm.

The trap's driver was a middle-aged man, broad-shouldered and big-handed, with the red nose of a drinker. He grinned and waved to Felton, who didn't respond.

'Who's that?' Pike asked.

'Trouble,' Felton said. 'Got plans for the evening, lad?'

'Well, no, not really—'

'That was a rhetorical question.' Felton turned and strode down the High Street. 'Come on. We have work to do.'

The clock ticked towards seven. Thirty men, the whole of Winchester's police force, stood shoulder to shoulder in the small police station that occupied one end of the Guildhall.

Felton surveyed his troops. 'I'm sorry to have to call everyone in like this. Hopefully, you won't be needed, but there's been ugly talk in the town, and we must be prepared.'

Pike glanced out of the window. People were gathering round the old Russian artillery piece, just outside the park near the statue of King Alfred. A loose crowd filled the Broadway, hundreds of people: working men and shopkeepers, women and children.

'Now,' Felton said, 'People have a right to hold a peaceful meeting, so let's not make trouble where there's none. As long as it's quiet, keep your heads down, but be ready to move in a hurry. Have your bicycles to hand. All right?'

The assembled policemen nodded.

'Right. Pike, you're with me.'

Pike gulped. 'What? Oh, right, sir.'

He followed Felton out of the station. They skirted the edge of the crowd.

'Sir, can I ask a question?' Pike dodged a pretty young woman, who smiled at him. 'What's all this about? The meeting, I mean?'

'Did you notice this morning the railings round the gun had been removed?'

'Uh...'

The old artillery piece was just a black, ugly lump of metal, relic of a long ago war, sitting on its gun carriage on a patch of gravel. It was just there, a familiar landmark not worth a second look.

'Observation, lad. Very useful skill. Council workmen removed the railings last night.' Felton stared into the throng of people. 'Those two are soldiers or I'll give you a shilling.'

Pike followed Felton's gaze, but wasn't sure who he was looking at. Soldiers from the barracks were often in town, but out of uniform, how would he know them?

'If there's trouble, the last thing we need is soldiers mixed in it.' Felton scanned the crowd. 'Do you see an MP anywhere?'

'A what?'

'Ah, there's one.' Felton strode away.

Pike followed, weaving between people to not lose sight of his boss. The crowd had grown and was still growing. There must be over a thousand now, and it felt like an election rally or a football match, the mood cheerful, excited, tense with expectation.

Trouble, Felton had said. Pike's heart bumped. What sort of trouble?

Felton had found a man in uniform. After a short conversation, the soldier headed into the crowd and Felton strolled back to Pike.

'Well, maybe that's one or two fewer problems,' Felton said. 'What time is it now?'

Pike glanced at the town clock. 'Nearly half seven.'

A trumpet blared. Everyone stirred at the sound, every head straining for a better view as a gang of men pushed through the crowd. In the lead was a young man with a cornet, and the stout red-faced character beside him was the man they'd seen earlier, driving the pony and trap.

'Say what you like about Joe, he knows how to make an entrance,' Felton said.

Cheers and clapping spread through the sea of people. The cornet player blew a fanfare.

'Who is he?'

'Joseph Dumper. Good old Joe,' Felton said sourly. 'Decent enough chap, when he's not drinking.'

Reaching the centre of the throng, Joe clambered onto the gun and stood upright in the middle, balancing with the ease of a strong, active man. The cornet player blew another fanfare and the crowd cheered.

Joe acknowledged them with a grin and a wave. 'Ladies and gentlemen, friends!'

He had a good speaking voice, loud and carrying. The crowd quieted.

'At the last meeting we agreed to send a protest,' Joe said. 'I handed that protest in the next day, and the Mayor acknowledged it. Now, that being so, the Mayor had no right, nor the Councillors had any right; they should have let well alone until the thing was settled.'

Cheers interrupted the speech. 'Hear, hear!'

Joe waved his hands until the crowd quieted. 'If the Council felt justified in what they were doing, why remove the railings at night? It puts me in mind of a midnight poacher or a burglar. The fact is, they totally ignored the citizen's wishes. Now, I ask you, are they fit to rule in this city?'

'No!' men shouted, followed by a blast on the cornet.

'This being our glorious Empire Day, only this afternoon our honourable mayor has been educating the children how to build an Empire; while last night, he taught us citizens how to pull down an Empire by taking away this protective barrier.'

'Hear, hear, Joe!'

'Good old Joe!'

'I gave reasons at the last meeting why they shouldn't remove those railings round this relic of the Crimean veterans. They say "Building an Empire"—where's the respect for the British Soldier?'

'They ain't got none!'

'Where's the respect for the British working man? They talk about the wage question—who do they pay? The man that gets £5 a week gets £7, but the man who gets 18s a week, he can get 16s.'

The crowd laughed and cheered. Pike caught himself nodding: his own father had often said something similar.

'The British working man, he stands on his own. If there's any gentleman of the Council can say anything contrary to what I've said, I challenge him to stand here and put it to you fair and square. I'd like to hear our worthy Mayor explain himself!'

'Hear, hear!'

Joe shook his fist. 'We are disgusted, disgusted, disgusted with this action. Don't you, one and all, condemn this action?'

'Yes,' the crowd roared back.

'I propose we make a demonstration through the city and leave no stone unturned to tell them.'

The cornet blared and the crowd whooped.

'Now we'll go round to the Mayor's house.'

Borne up on a wave of cheers, Joe seated himself on the shoulders of two young men.

'Joe, Joe!' a thousand voices cried in unison. Carrying Joe at their head, the whole mob surged up the street, their shouts and cheers merging into a roar.

Felton seized Pike's arm and drew him close enough to speak without shouting. 'Nip back to the station, lad,' he said calmly. 'Get ten men on their bikes to the Mayor's house, quick as they can.'

After the fervid atmosphere of the crowd, walking into the relative quiet of the station was like being doused with cold water. Pike shivered under the steady gaze of Sergeant Day. 'Sarge, the boss wants ten men to the Mayor's house, quick.'

The sergeant eyed him. 'Well, you're one. Get your bike, lad.'

A few minutes later, out of breath from the short bike race, Pike and nine other constables stood in a line in front of the Mayor's house. When they arrived, Felton had spoken to someone inside. The lights had hurriedly been dowsed, and now the house stood silent, every window dark and curtained.

Joe and his supporters had gone through Cross Keys Passage, and slowed by the bottleneck, the crowd had strung out. The waiting policemen heard them advancing up Silver Hill with shouts and cheers and repeated blasts from the cornet.

Joe arrived first, still sitting on the shoulders of his supporters with the cornet player alongside, then gangs of boys and young working men. At the sight of the police they halted, bunching up as hundreds of people flowed in behind.

Pike trembled. Listening to Joe speak, he'd been caught up in the crowd's excitement and if he hadn't been in uniform, he would have joined them. It felt very different to be one of ten policemen facing that same crowd.

Felton advanced to meet them. 'What do you want, Joe?'

'We want a word with the Mayor. Won't you tell him to come out?'

His gang laughed. 'The Mayor! Let's see the Mayor.'

'He's not in,' Felton said.

'Let's have the Mayor!' someone yelled.

A stone cracked into a window. Pike flinched at the sharp noise. A boy—a lad not much younger than himself—took another stone from his pocket and flung it. Shards of glass crashed to the pavement, and the young men cheered.

'Enough of that.' Felton's voice cut through the noise of the crowd. 'You've made your point. Go home now, why don't you? The Mayor's not here.'

The bulk of the crowd had now caught up with the leaders. Bodies packed the street like sardines in a can.

Many hands helped Joe stand, balanced on the shoulders of his supporters. He faced his audience. 'The reason we've gathered here, outside his Worship's residence, is to condemn the Council's action in removing the railings. The Mayor's not here, but let him be in no doubt: there'll be no rest until the railings are put back.'

Joe jumped down, and with a wave of his arm and a blare from the cornet, the crowd moved on. They flowed up Silver Hill past the policemen, jeering and cat-calling as they went.

Felton gestured to Pike's end of the line. 'Right, you five on bikes. The rest of you stay here.'

They'd stashed the bikes down the side of the house, out of sight. Pike and the other four men fetched theirs.

Further up the road, the crowd erupted into cheers, accompanied by the crash and tinkle of broken glass. Pike gripped the handlebars of his bike, exchanging glances with his companions. *Five of us,* he thought. Just five policemen against thousands; he didn't know whether to laugh or cower in terror.

Felton mounted his bike. 'Ready?' He eyed his small contingent, his gaze lingering on Pike.

Pike squared his shoulders. He was the youngest and least experienced, but he was no coward. Whatever Felton and the others could do, so could he.

'Right. Stick together and follow me.'

Felton wobbled off, weaving between the stragglers from the mob, and Pike fell in behind, peddling with grim determination.

The mob passed along North Walls and back by Jewry Street, breaking every street lamp on the way, then down the High Street. The big windows of the George Hotel made an irresistible target: glass smashed and the crowd yelled approval. Thousands of excited people converged toward the Broadway and the Guildhall. Stones whizzed overhead and glass rained down from the street lamps. The town clock came under fire.

Someone shouted: 'What about the Pageant grounds?'

The crowd cheered and in a mass, set out for Wolvesey Castle. Along the way, they tore up two benches from the

Broadway and bore them triumphantly overhead. Loud splashes and cheers signalled the benches being thrown in the river.

On their bicycles, the handful of policemen could only trail in the wake of chaos.

'We need to get ahead of them,' Felton shouted.

The little band of policemen peddled hard, dodging the crowd and diving into the narrow back-streets. Pike's teeth juddered as they cycled over the cobbles.

The mob reached the gates first. They were locked, but that meant nothing against hundreds of determined men. They simply pushed until sheer weight of bodies broke the gates from their hinges. With a roar, the crowd trampled through into the grounds, where the grandstand for next month's pageant stood against the backdrop of the ruined palace. Preparations for the event had been going on for months.

'Shouldn't we do something, sir?' Pike asked.

'Do you have a suggestion?' Felton replied dryly.

A discordant jangle came from an overturned piano. On the other side of the site, a gang of men seized on a mocked-up chariot and dragged it toward the gates, shouting for Joe.

'Look out. They're on the move again,' Felton said.

Capricious as children, the mob had lost interest in wrecking the Pageant props. Now they wanted Joe to sit in the chariot so they could drag him through the town like a Roman emperor in his triumph.

This plan too was short-lived. When the chariot reached the bridge, someone yelled, 'Chuck it in.'

Many hands hoisted the timber-and-canvas chariot over the rail. It splashed into the river below and they cheered as if they'd won a football match.

The mob returned to the Broadway and surrounded the old gun.

'Joe needs a carriage.' Shouts and laughter. 'Get some ropes!'

Ropes appeared from somewhere and were tied round the gun.

'All together now — heave!'

The gun rocked and tipped. The thud of its fall shook the ground, celebrated with more cheers and laughter.

Pike felt sick. Many of the rioters were drinking, but alcohol wasn't enough to fuel this senseless destruction. They were drunk on their own wildness, mad with anarchy. In this mood, they might do anything.

Joe perched on the gun carriage and pointed up the High Street. 'Onward!'

With wild yells, the mob surged round the gun carriage and dragged it, and Joe, up the street.

In Mayor Forder's drawing room, the clock on the mantle ticked towards eleven. From the front of the house came the muffled rattle of stones striking brickwork. The Mayor winced at the sound.

All the windows were already broken. He hated to think how much it would cost to fix the damage. But of course, his own house wasn't the only victim. The ruffians had broken street lamps and windows all over town.

His wife Ada sat with her hands clenched in her lap, her face pale.

Alderman Carter stood by the fireplace, rocking on his heels. 'It's a bad business, very bad. Will we need to read the Riot Act? Do you think?'

'No, no. I've sent Mr Fear to the barracks with a letter requesting assistance. As Chief Magistrate, I'm quite entitled to do that.'

'But don't you need to read the Riot Act, if we bring the soldiers in?'

The Mayor took a deep breath ready to explain exactly what he thought of the Riot Act, but was interrupted by the arrival of Councillor Fear. The man's name had never been more appropriate; he was visibly trembling.

'Mr Mayor,' he blurted. 'The mob are coming back down Edgar Road. They've been to Anderson's house, broken every window! They say his little boy's bed was covered with stones.'

Ada gasped.

'Good heavens. Is anyone hurt?' Carter said.

'Not as far as I know, no, but the crowd are heading back this way. What are we to do?'

The Mayor stared at him. They all looked to him as if he ought to know, but what could he do? Thousands of men were rampaging through the town, howling for his blood. When they'd gathered outside his house with only a handful of policemen to hold them off, he was sure his time had come. What had he ever done to deserve this? This nonsense about the gun wasn't even his fault, he'd had nothing to do with it. He'd always tried to help the poor.

And this was how they thanked him. There was only one option: he'd have to call in the army to restore order. What else could do?

He flinched at another thump from the front of the house. Only the front door slamming, he realised.

The maid showed in a tall, red-faced man, all bristling moustache and uniform. The Mayor had a moment to recognise Major Warde, Chief Constable of Hampshire, before he erupted. 'What the devil are you doing here, Forder? Your place is at the Guildhall. This mess is entirely your fault. Why aren't you addressing the people? Why haven't you sworn in special constables?'

'Major Warde.' Pulling himself together, the Mayor gestured to the settee. 'Will you sit down?'

The Chief Constable scowled. 'No, I will not.'

'If you would just discuss the situation calmly, I'm sure we'd be glad of your advice—'

'Your duty is at the Guildhall. Please go and do it.'

Pinned in the Major's glare, the Mayor squirmed. The Chief Constable of Hampshire had no jurisdiction in the city, and certainly no right to barge into a man's own home and bark orders. He had half a mind to say so quite firmly, then he caught Ada's eye. A glance from her, a slight frown, was all that was needed. His protest withered unspoken.

In a way, it was a relief to be told what to do, however rudely the suggestion was made. 'Well, very well, I'll go with you.' He squared his shoulders. He was Mayor, after all. It was his duty to be courageous, to go to the Guildhall, to address the baying mob in all the dignity of his office. Yes, it was his duty. He would go, and show Major Warde that bravery wasn't restricted to men of aristocratic birth and Army careers. 'We had better go in the back way.'

Major Warde sneered. 'Do as you like. I am not accustomed to using back doors.'

A swaying mass of humanity flooded the Broadway in front of the Guildhall. Boos and shouts and stamping feet made a single roar of sound, punctuated by stones rattling off buildings and the smash of glass. In the lampless night, it was impossible to guess their numbers. There must have been thousands.

A line of twelve policemen stood in front of the police station, including Constable Pike. They'd been issued with staves—long, sturdy sticks—in place of the usual truncheons. Pike couldn't say it gave him much comfort.

A councillor appeared on the Guildhall's balcony and tried to address the crowd, but his voice was lost in the maelstrom.

'The Mayor!' the cry went up, 'Bring out the Mayor.'

The Mayor shuffled onto the balcony with other councillors behind him. He raised his hands and his mouth moved, but whatever he said went unheard in the sea of noise.

'Quiet.' Joe's bellow carried over the noise of the crowd. 'Let's hear what he has to say.'

Lifted above the crowd, Joe staggered from shoulder to shoulder to reach the Guildhall steps, cheered all the way. He climbed onto the stone balustrade and stood there, poised, looking up at the Mayor. The Mayor leaned over the balcony railing to speak to him.

Joe waved to the crowd. 'The Mayor says he undertakes, on behalf of the Council, that the railings will be put back.'

Cheers rang out. Joe slipped down from his perch into the arms of his friends.

Pike sighed. Surely now, sanity would be restored. But his relief was short-lived: the bulk of the crowd either hadn't heard or didn't care. More stones flew.

A knot of well-dressed, older men emerged from the Guildhall and scuttled down the steps toward the police station, among them the Mayor. The crowd howled. Someone in the front ranks hurled a piece of timber. It crashed into a window feet from the Mayor's head. With a terrified yelp, he bolted for the police line.

The crowd surged forward. In the front row, a hatless man held a bottle. Another wielded a length of black iron railing like a spear. Mouths gaped, shouting words lost in the noise, flushed faces wild and inhuman.

Pike gripped his stave hard, trying to stop himself shaking. Twelve policemen were all that stood between the mob and their prey. Long sticks or not, the vast crowd would trample them and tear the Mayor to pieces.

'Draw staves,' Felton ordered.

Pike lifted his stick, and as he stared into the eyes of the charging rioters, he saw the moment of doubt, of hesitation.

One slowed, then another, and the crowd piled on itself, and stopped, and backed away.

Numb with relief, Pike clung to his stave as a drowning man clutches a lifeline. It was like, he thought, one man facing down a herd of cows. Though each animal is more than capable of flattening him, none of them dare, and as long as he shows no fear they must give way.

The rioters didn't know the terror knotting his guts, or that he'd only used the stave in drill. All they saw was the uniforms, and the staves, and that the men holding them stood firm, and, thank God, that had been enough.

Pike glanced at his colleagues: pale, as he must be, but resolute, and he stood his ground with new conviction.

Behind him, the panting Mayor had reached Felton. 'May I—May I use your telephone, Head Constable?'

Behind cracked glass, the hands of the town clock edged toward midnight. Strange tides drove the crowd. Now they rushed the Guildhall, and the next moment charged the police station, only to fall back, milling in confusion. No one knew what was happening, no one was in charge.

Rumour said troops had mustered outside the City Arms Hotel. The crowd pulled in on itself, shrinking, and perhaps some chose that moment to sidle away, unnoticed in the dark.

But no soldiers came. According to another rumour, Major Warde had sent them back.

'For the best,' Sergeant Day said.

Pike only wanted the night to end. Each fresh alarm cut through his tiredness, and when the threat passed exhaustion crashed down like a hammer, leaving him drained and shaky. 'But if the soldiers come down, the rioters will go home, won't they?'

'Think, lad,' Day said. 'Yes, they might run at the first sight of guns. But a mob don't always do what you expect.

What if they fight? What if someone's killed? The soldiers *live* in this town. They drink in the pubs, they walk the streets every day. No, we don't want that sort of trouble, not if we can help it.'

Soldiers firing on the crowd… Pike shuddered. It surely wouldn't, couldn't come to that. For all the noise and commotion and window-breaking, as far as he knew, not a single man had been hurt.

A chorus of booing and another rush on Guildhall greeted the appearance of the Mayor on the balcony. He was trying to speak again, appealing for calm and for the crowd to go home.

'Read the Riot Act!' someone yelled, drawing laughter. 'Riot Act, Riot Act,' the crowd chanted.

Red in the face, the Mayor withdrew.

Mayor Forder ran the gauntlet again, scuttling down the steps of the Guildhall to the police station in the face of the laughing, shouting, booing mob.

He stepped through the line of policemen into the shelter of the station. 'May I use your telephone, Head Constable?'

The policemen avoided meeting his eye. Sniggering behind their carefully blank faces, he was sure, and it was all Warde's fault. He'd made the Mayor a laughing stock. He half-expected to see Felton sneer, but his expression and manner were respectful as ever.

'Carry on, sir. You know the way.'

Alone in the office, the Mayor snatched up the telephone. It shook in his hand. He clutched it to his chest, taking several deep breaths to regain his composure before he made the call.

'Hello? Hello? This is the Mayor, for the Officer Commanding.'

'Oh, excuse me...' The voice on the other end spoke muffled words to someone else. 'Lord Henniker is just coming, if you don't mind waiting a moment.'

He waited, fuming. It was more than a moment before the telephone changed hands, and Lord Henniker's aristocratic drawl came down the wire from the barracks. 'Ah, your Worship? Can I assist you in some way?'

The Mayor drew himself up. 'Are you, or are you not, going to bring your men down to stop this riot?'

'Major Warde says you don't want them.'

'I do want them. As Chief Magistrate, I require the military to come down and restore order in the streets.'

'I've brought them down twice tonight. I shan't bring them down again.'

Twice! The Mayor closed his eyes. That damn interfering Warde. Who did he think he was, sending the soldiers back when the Mayor had asked for them? It was outrageous. 'I mean to report this matter to the proper authorities.'

'Do so,' Lord Henniker replied, followed by a click.

'Are you there? Hello?'

No answer came. The Mayor slammed the telephone down on the desk.

As the night drew on, fatigue overtook excitement and the crowd thinned until only the police remained, watching a few persistent loiterers.

Felton gathered the constables in the station. 'It's over for the night, I think. You've done well. I'm proud of you all.'

The Head Constable's eyes were tired, but every exhausted man stood a little straighter under his gaze.

'I don't expect there'll be more trouble tonight, but I must ask for a few volunteers to stay in case anything happens.'

Sergeant Day raised his hand, and Jones who'd been one of the five on their bikes, and Daniels who'd stood beside

Pike to face the rioter's charge, and more than half the rest of the men. Pike, feeling lightheaded, lifted his hand too.

Felton smiled. 'Thank you. Five men will be enough. This isn't over, and I want you rested for tomorrow.'

Relieved from duty, Pike walked back to his lodgings through the dark city. Broken glass crunched underfoot. These streets should be quiet at night, quiet with the domestic peace of sleeping families, but this was a different quiet: the tense, huddled silence of uncertainty and fear.

The city woke to the damage done by the riot. Shock gave way to annoyance. Shopkeepers tutted and swept glass from the pavements. Workmen boarded broken windows. The effects of the night's anarchy couldn't be washed away in a moment, but hour by hour the destruction was tamed, the streets reclaimed by normality.

The cause of it all, the gun, lay on its side near the abandoned gun carriage. Here people gathered to stare, shake their heads, and exchange the latest gossip.

Mid-morning, Good Old Joe himself sauntered up to inspect his handiwork. From his post outside the police station, Pike noted several other men whose faces he recognised from the night before.

He pointed them out to Felton. 'I'm sure I saw that man throwing stones. Should we arrest him?'

'If there's any arresting to do, lad, I'll let you know. But I will have a word with them.'

The Head Constable ambled over to the gathering. Felton met Joe. After a short exchange of words, they nodded, and Joe left.

Pike watched and wondered. Last night, the mob had been lawless vandals, and this morning those same men walked the streets, unafraid and unashamed. He'd always thought criminals skulked in dark alleys, but who here was a criminal and who a law-abiding citizen? And why wouldn't Felton arrest them? Surely he ought to arrest criminals and put them in prison—otherwise, what were the police for?

Later a group of men, including some Pike recognised as rioters, brought ropes and tried to get the gun back on its carriage. Last night it had been tipped over easily. Setting it right proved harder, mainly because the many helpers all had different ideas of how to proceed. As a result, the gun went nowhere.

Pike shook his head. It was certainly a funny old world.

In the afternoon, council workmen remounted the gun on its carriage and returned it to its usual place. Crowds came to gawk at the damage.

Speculation, rumour, and gossip heated the air. Everyone knew there would be trouble. Though the Mayor had repeated his promise to have the railings replaced, everyone expected—had heard a rumour, had overheard a man in a pub say—there would be trouble.

As evening drew on the crowd in front of the Guildhall grew, the atmosphere as yet more curious than angry. By nine o'clock, thousands again filled the Broadway, shouting and booing and heckling the police. Scuffles broke out in the crowd.

Inside the Guildhall, Mayor Forder huddled with the councillors. 'I'll address the crowd. I'll tell them to go home.'

Alderman Carter nodded. Councillor Fear smiled approvingly.

The Mayor swallowed. 'Right. I'll go, shall I?' He searched the faces of his colleagues, half-hoping one would restrain him, but no one said anything, so he turned to the front doors. 'Right. I'm going.'

It was some reassurance that he'd sworn in hundreds of special constables during the day. Though on Felton's advice most were marshalled in a yard behind the Guildhall, out of sight. The Mayor would have preferred them lined up in front of the Guildhall, especially right now.

Pulling himself up to his full, if rather unimpressive, height, he stepped through the door to a chorus of boos. He raised his hands, appealing for silence, and after a few minutes, the crowd quieted enough for him to speak.

He cleared his throat. 'Citizens, I appeal to you to go home quietly, for the good of the city you love. You have no grievance. Go home peacefully and protect your homes and children. I do appeal to you very much indeed. Why make this demonstration?'

A woman shouted, 'Who started it?'

'I didn't start it at all,' the Mayor said. 'You've got your railings and your gun. Let me ask you: who looked after the unemployed?'

Boos and cheers answered him.

'Who looked after the schoolchildren?' the Mayor said. 'Who had Empire Day celebrations?'

'Not you!'

'Who moved the railings in the middle of the night?' a man shouted.

Another yelled: 'We'll have King Alfred down before we're done.'

'I had nothing to do with the railings,' the Mayor said. Which was true: he'd been in favour of removing the wretched railings, but he hadn't ordered the work done. If he'd known about it, he would have stopped it. But he hadn't. None of this was his fault.

A fight broke out in front of the Guildhall just below him. A portion of the crowd rushed the police station.

The Mayor flushed. Thousands of people were laughing and jeering and ignoring him, and he was helpless, in his own city, his own Guildhall.

'Show us the special constables,' someone shouted from the crowd. 'Bring out England's Last Hope.'

More laughter, and amid the general uproar, one section of the crowd cheered. Attention shifted; now the whole crowd was applauding and whistling, and it wasn't for the Mayor. Joseph Dumper was climbing onto the balustrade.

'Good old Joe,' went up the cry, and 'Show us the special constables!'

The Mayor smiled. After two miserable days of humiliation at the hands of Joe Dumper and his mob and Major Warde and his soldier cronies, his moment had come. He pointed to Joe. 'You want to see special constables? Here's one.'

Joe raised his hands for quiet. 'Citizens!' His bellow silenced the crowd. 'I hope and trust you'll do everything in your power to maintain order, because you've got all you asked for.'

'We haven't got the railings up yet,' someone shouted back.

'Take my advice and go home peacefully,' Joe said.

Two of Joe's cronies at the front of the crowd clambered up to join him.

'Let's have the song of the Old Brigade!' one shouted.

'Order, order,' the Mayor said. 'What Mr Dumper said is quite true. I gave you a promise last night, and the Council have supported me this morning. The railings will be replaced. Now go home and don't make any more disturbances. I appeal to you. You are all sensible men and women. Do your duty and protect your city.'

'Now, gentlemen,' Joe said. 'Three cheers for the Mayor!'

The crowd cheered and booed.

'Three cheers for Joe Dumper!' someone yelled, to general laughter.

'Now go home like good boys,' Joe said. 'Or I'll have nothing more to do with you.'

After the speeches by the Mayor and Joe Dumper, the mood of the crowd turned jovial and many went home. As the battered town clock ticked toward midnight, the mob had thinned into straggling groups of trouble-makers.

At his post in the police station, Pike began to hope the business would soon end.

Felton appeared in the doorway, supporting a man who seemed to have difficulty standing. Pike jumped to his feet.

'This here is Mr Mattock,' Felton said.

'I like you, Mr Felton,' Mattock slurred. 'I'm very pleased you're going to lock me up.'

Felton patted him on the back. 'Sergeant Day, would you mind seeing Mr Mattock to a cell? I don't think he'll be any trouble.'

Sergeant Day pried Mattock away from Felton and steered him toward the cells.

Outside the police station, a scuffle had broken out. A man charged through the doorway and ploughed into Pike, head first. Pike staggered. The man fastened his teeth in the thick material of Pike's sleeve.

It was the first time Pike had been hit in the line of duty. He dredged his brain for any words of wisdom from his brief training. Nothing sprang to mind, so he simply punched his attacker in the jaw, quite hard.

The man crumpled to the floor. 'Ow,' he said. 'You hit me.'

Pike seized his arm and hauled him upright. 'You're under arrest.' He looked to Felton. 'Is that all right, sir?'

Felton smiled. 'Quite all right. Carry on, Constable.'

His prisoner stared at Pike, round-eyed. Though stinking of beer, he looked a respectable tradesman. The riot had swept up all sorts of people besides the usual trouble-makers.

Pike gripped his prize, wondering what to do. He'd never arrested anyone. Indeed, he realised with a glow of pride, he'd just made his first arrest. In two days and hectic nights, he'd turned from a boy in a policeman's uniform into a real policeman.

Finally the Broadway was empty of all but a handful of drunks. The usual nighttime quiet slunk back into place. The riot was over.

The special constables were dismissed, never having been called on. They departed, chatting over the day's events as they spread out into the sleeping town.

'What do we do now, sir?' Pike asked Felton. Despite his second late night in a row, he still buzzed with the excitement of his first arrest.

'I don't know about you, lad, but I haven't taken this uniform off in the best part of two days, so I'm for home, a bath, dinner, and bed. Not necessarily in that order.' Felton nodded to Sergeant Day. 'Carry on, Sergeant.'

Sergeant Day saluted. Pike and he watched the Head Constable stroll across the Broadway.

'Great man, that is,' the sergeant said. 'Who'd have thought of signing Joe Dumper as a special constable? Clever, very clever.' He shook his head. 'Word of advice, lad. Take Mr Felton as your model and you'll not go far wrong.'

Pike gazed out at the dishevelled street. Only empty bottles and paper bags and broken glass remained as evidence of what had passed in the last few hours. In a few days, or weeks at most, the damage would be fixed, and the whole extraordinary business brushed up and forgotten, perhaps.

But he'd never forget standing with a handful of men, facing down a crowd of thousands with nothing but a stick. He'd never forget the wildness of the mob, the senseless destruction that could so easily have flashed into bloodshed. And he'd never forget Head Constable Felton, the calm leadership which had somehow anchored them all.

'Thanks, Sarge,' Pike said. 'I'll do my best.'

HISTORICAL NOTE

This story is closely based on contemporary newspaper reports of the riot, which include the speeches and even details of some private conversations. Beyond that, though the principal characters are all real people, their thoughts and motivations are invented. There was a Police Constable Pike who subdued and arrested a drunk, but since I had no other information about him, his character and role in events is entirely fictional.

Saving the Cathedral

Maggie Farran

The historical pageant in 1908 raised £2000 for vital ongoing repairs to the cathedral, which were particularly challenging because the cathedral's foundations are mostly under water.

William Walker walked stiffly with the weight of his diving suit and boots slowing his pace considerably. He looked forward to his lunch hour when he could enjoy fresh air, and today, a little sunshine. He lifted off his helmet and delighted in the feel of the breeze on his face.

He smoked his pipe, hoping it would kill off any germs from the deep water. He smiled and relaxed. Today was Friday and so after his afternoon shift he would be cycling home to South Norwood. He so looked forward to his weekends when he was reunited with his wife and children. He relished those two days of normal family life each week. On Monday he would be back in Winchester again to do his vital work to save the ancient cathedral from collapse.

After his lunch he replaced his helmet and returned to the job that had been his for the last few years since 1906.

He dived down thirteen feet into the cloudy, muddy water beneath the cathedral. It smelt strongly of peat. He had to work in total darkness and feel his way around.

His job was the same every day. He had to place bags of concrete underwater to build a new foundation to support the cathedral walls. He had been a deep sea diver in Portsmouth when Francis Fox, a civil engineer, had contacted him with his strange request.

'I need an experienced diver like you, William, to save Winchester Cathedral from collapsing. Huge cracks have appeared in the walls and ceiling. Some of them are large enough for owls to roost in. Chunks of stone are falling to the ground.'

William had been interested in the job as it sounded such a challenge and he felt it would be an honour to be part of saving a beautiful old building.

'What would I have to do? I don't really understand why you need a diver to save the cathedral.'

'Well, Thomas Jackson, the architect, wants to underpin the medieval south and east walls with modern new foundations. When the cathedral was expanded in the 13th century beech logs were used as foundation. Over the years they have been inadequate. The walls have started to lean outwards and rotate. We need new strong concrete foundations.'

William found his work totally absorbing. The concentration needed to work in darkness was like meditating. He could think of nothing else and relied completely on his sense of touch. He felt alone and oblivious to any problems of the world above the darkness of the water. Yet he knew his very life depended upon the men above the surface of the water who were keeping him alive by operating the diving pump which ensured his vital air supply.

He had been underwater for about an hour when he began to feel slightly anxious. It was not sudden but a gradual feeling that he was finding it slightly more difficult to breathe. At first he thought he was imagining it. He knew his mind could play all kinds of tricks when he was tired and coming towards the end of the week. The water was so murky his vivid imagination had conjured up all kinds of mythical creatures swimming towards him through the peaty water. He was always able to dismiss anything he thought he saw. He would absorb himself in his work and talk sternly to himself.

'Get on with the job, William, there is nothing under here but you and this cloudy water.'

However this time it was not working. He was finding it hard to breathe and his heart was pumping at a furious speed. He was feeling uncomfortably warm and he was shaking slightly. He would like to surface but he hadn't been diving long enough for another break so soon after his lunch break. He tried to calm himself down again.

'Pull yourself together, William, you are imagining all these symptoms. You've been doing this job for a long time now. You want to get it finished don't you? After all you are saving the cathedral from collapse. You can't give into your silly imaginings.'

Then he saw him. Another diver was swimming toward him through the haze. As the diver got nearer William could see that he wore no diving suit or breathing apparatus. There was a golden light around him and strange purple stars twinkling all around him. The peaty smell had vanished and had been replaced by a beautiful scent that reminded William of walking through a pine forest when he was a boy. The other diver stopped a few inches from his face and spoke in a low clear voice.

'My dear friend, William, I want to thank you for saving my house. You have been working tirelessly for all these years in these awful conditions. You have shown such dedication. You will be rewarded. I will not forget you.'

William immediately felt wrapped in joy. His heart stopped beating so fast and his breath steadied. All the fear he had felt left him. As he watched, the strange diver swam away and disappeared from view. The golden light and the purple stars were the last to vanish. He found he was able to carry on his work quite calmly again. He was so sure of the strange things he had seen and heard and yet he knew he would share them with no one except his wife when he got home. His wife would believe him and best of all she would not think he had been driven mad by his difficult yet monotonous job.

When he surfaced at the end of his shift, the two men who operated the diving pump which ensured his vital air supply both shook his hand and looked relieved.

'How are you feeling, William? We had a bit of trouble with the pump. It didn't seem to be working properly. We nearly had to get you out quickly. It seemed to be blocked somehow, but anyway it righted itself in a few minutes and so we just carried on.'

William laughed 'Oh, I'm fine. Glad you sorted it out. I did feel a bit short of breath at one point but the feeling didn't last for long.'

He removed his boots, helmet, and diving suit with the help of his dresser. He was two hundred pounds lighter and he relished the feeling of freedom.

After a snack and a short rest he started his long cycle ride to South Norwood. His wife and children would be waiting for him at home. He loved them dearly and his weekends were precious family time. However he found the demands on him personally quite hard to adjust to. His children were noisy and would all talk to him all at once. His wife always had a list of jobs lined up for him to complete over the weekend. He relished the long cycle home as a bridge between the solitariness of his diving and his large noisy family.

As he got into the rhythm of his cycling he allowed himself to think about his wife and what he was going to tell her about the underwater vision. She would love hearing about the mysterious diver and what he had said. It would be more interesting to her than the usual tales of peaty water and underwater darkness. He pedalled a little faster. He couldn't wait to see her.

HISTORICAL NOTE

From 1906, William Walker, an experienced diver, worked under water below the cathedral for six hours a day in depths up to 6 metres. He worked in total darkness, using his bare hands to feel his way through the cloudy, muddy water. It took him six years to excavate the flooded trenches and fill them with bags of concrete.

A special service of thanksgiving was held on St Swithun's Day 1912, after which Walker was presented with a silver rose bowl by King George V.

There is a statue of him just before you reach the Cathedral café.

Reflection

Maggie Farran

After over one thousand years of building, destruction, and reconstruction, Winchester Cathedral remains the heart of the city and a haven for troubled souls, whatever their religious beliefs.

Rose and her mother chose a little round table for two by the tall flint wall. It was set slightly away from the rest of the tables outside the Cathedral Café. It offered them the privacy they needed.

'It's so lovely and warm sitting by this wall. I know it's a beautiful sunny day, but the wall shelters you. I just want to soak in all this sunshine after the cold winter we've had. Hold my hand, darling. Let's try to enjoy our cakes before we get into our real discussion,' said her mother in her gentle voice.

Rose reached over and held her mother's hand. She wished she was seven again. She just wanted her mother to make the decision for her, but she knew it had to be hers alone.

She sipped her Earl Grey tea and took a bite from her slice of coffee and walnut cake.

Her mother was wearing a pretty summer dress. It suited her so well with its bright red poppy heads on a white background. Her smooth hair glinted with shades of golden brown.

Her mother looked at her with her kind eyes that seemed to be able to look into her soul. 'The cakes here are so delicious. How's your cake, Rose? My chocolate cake is heavenly.'

Rose tried to swallow, but the cake just seemed to stay in her mouth. She washed it down with some tea. 'I'm sure it's lovely, Mum, but I can't seem to concentrate on anything else now. I just don't know what to do. One moment I think one thing and then I think another.'

'Darling, you know I'd do anything to help you, but it has to be your decision. You have to live with it.'

Rose stroked her tiny bump and shivered. She felt so cold, for a moment, despite the glorious sunny day. She had been so happy to be pregnant. She had wanted a baby since she was a little girl. Now everything was spoilt.

She had been so excited to have her scan. She had asked her mother to come with her to see her grandchild for the first time. They had both known something was wrong when the sonographer suddenly went quiet. Now she was faced with this terrible decision. It was so unfair.

Rose forced down her last bit of cake. She turned to her mother, looking directly into her dove-grey eyes. 'Mum, what would you do? I know it's an unfair question, but I just want to know what decision you would have made.'

Her mother took her hand again and squeezed it lovingly.

'Darling, remember you were my baby and I will always love you whatever you decide. I know I couldn't have managed to look after a handicapped baby, but you're stronger than me. We aren't the same person. I've always admired your spirit. You take after Dad in that way. I wish he was still here. He was always so wise and kind.'

They both looked down at the table and fiddled with the cake crumbs left on their plates. Rose missed her father terribly, but she knew it was far worse for her mother. She felt selfish burdening her mother with her problems.

'Mum, I'm so sorry. Let's talk about something else. I should be talking to Richard, but he'll say it's up to me. I know him well enough after four years. He'll say that it's me that has to go through the pregnancy and give birth. He would never oppose any decision I made about our baby.'

A toddler with a mass of red curly hair crashed into their table. One of the cups fell to the ground and smashed. He looked up at Rose and started to cry, frightened by what he had done. A young woman rushed to their table.

'Charlie, what have you done? I told you not to rush about.' She turned to Rose. 'I'm so sorry. Are you alright?' She looked at Rose's little bump 'I hope you don't mind me saying, but you'll soon know what it's like. He drives me mad, but I wouldn't be without him for a minute. Do you know what you're having? Is it a boy or a girl?'

Rose smiled 'It's a girl. I've just had my scan and found out.' She didn't tell her what else she had been told.

'Good luck then. Hope all goes well for you.'

'Thanks, I've been told girls are easier than boys, but I don't know how true that is.'

Rose and her mother got up without speaking and walked into the cathedral grounds. It was a happy scene with lots of people sitting on the grass enjoying the sunshine. Some were having picnics in little family groups and others were quietly reading in shady areas beneath the trees. Toddlers were squealing and running around the trees. A young couple were walking hand in hand reading the inscriptions on the gravestones.

They walked into the coolness of the cathedral and sat side by side on a pew at the back. They gazed up at the amazing ceiling and the splendour of the ancient Gothic building. Rose felt a new calmness wrap around her like a silk scarf. Her mother knelt down on one of the beautifully embroidered kneelers and closed her eyes in prayer.

Rose left her mother and walked down into the crypt. She was mesmerised by the mysterious life-sized statue of a solitary man contemplating the water held in his cupped hand. He was reflected in the shallow water beneath him. His dark face was bowed down in deep concentration as if he were meditating on the water. The black lead statue was set off by the honey-coloured arches of the crypt. Rose was alone and she felt a strange connection to the statue as if he were speaking to her.

She whispered to the lonely man before her. 'Tell me what to do? I haven't long to make this terrible decision.'

She waited for a long time and let her imagination work freely on the two different futures in front of her. She pondered whether she had enough love and patience to cope with a child with special needs. She imagined another future where this needy child did not exist.

She felt her body tingle and it was as if her doubts were flushed away. She knew what she was going to do. She felt at peace with herself.

Slowly she walked up the steps and back into the main cathedral building. She walked over to her mother and whispered, 'I'm going to keep her.'

Her mother nodded and smiled. She put her arm around Rose's shoulder. 'Are you sure darling? Is this what you really want?'

'I've never been so sure of anything in my life, Mum.'

They walked together out of the veiled light of the cathedral into the bright summer day.

* * *

NOTE

In the Cathedral Crypt there is a life-size statue of a man by the sculptor Antony Gormley. It is called Sound 11 and fashioned from lead out of a plaster cast of the artist's own body. The statue is of a man contemplating the water held in his cupped hands.

Lavender's Blue

Sally Howard

A short drive from Winchester, the beautiful gardens of the National Trust property Mottisfont Abbey are a great place to relax and unwind.

Oh dear, no chairs left!

Ally stepped into the kitchen garden at Montisfont Abbey, pulling her sunglasses off the top of her head. The heat was intense, bouncing off the brick walls which enclosed the herb beds and grassy areas. The other mums-to-be, who'd arrived in good time, had bagged all the chairs at the café, which stood alongside one of the stone walls.

I'm such a wooz, Ally thought, 'coz if I don't sit down soon, I'm gonna fall down!

'Over here, over here! But excuse me if I don't get up,' said Fi, laughing. She was stretched on a recliner, a sparkling glass of juice resting on her very pregnant tummy.

Fi waved her to a spare chair by the lavender bushes. Great, Ally thought, the bushes are alive with wasps. A lemony smell of lavender wafted over to her. It was soporific; she yawned as she watched a wasp land lazily on a purple head of lavender which bowed gracefully under its weight.

She eased her cumbersome frame onto the foldaway chair, hoping it wouldn't give way. Fi passed her a paper plate with a ham sandwich on it. Wasps and ham—recipe for disaster. How she hated wasps. She'd been stung once as a girl and had nearly fainted.

Fi interrupted her thoughts: 'Any sign yet?'

Fi was the only one of their expectant mother group to have had a baby before. Chloe and Thandie were first-timers. Ally's due date was first of all of them.

'Yes, anything yet? Due date tomorrow—exciting!' squeaked Chloe, pulling her chair round.

Exciting? She could hardly call it that. Nervous as anything, more like. She wondered how she was going to cope. Weren't the calming hormones meant to be kicking in around now, relaxing and preparing her for the imminent arrival? She remembered last night at the birthing class. It'd been hot and stuffy in the room at the doctor's surgery. The midwife had explained things in far too much detail—even showing pictures! It was all too much. She'd ended up sitting on the steps outside, breathing into a paper bag. Oh dear, she was such a wooz.

She smiled brightly: 'Nothing yet.'

'Let us know the first sign of anything.' Thandie put her hand on her arm. 'We'll be there to help.'

Suddenly Ally felt a smarting in her finger. She sat up sharply and the paper plate fell to the floor.

'Ow,' she said.

'You alright?' Fi rolled over to retrieve her plate.

'Darn wasp got me,' she said, looking down at her finger. A tiny black barb stuck out from her skin. She felt a wave of heat wash over her which had nothing to do with the weather. She had a strong urge to go home and lie down.

Instead, carefully, breathing deeply, she hooked her nail under it and tweezered it out.

'Ow,' she said again.

'Let me get you something for that,' said Fi, hoisting herself off her chair. 'You're not allergic or anything, are you?'

'Well, not normally, but I'm not so sure, being pregnant, you know.' Fi looked at her anxiously. 'No, I feel alright, really.'

Fi started rifling through her voluminous bag. Ally looked over at Fi's son and a school friend of his racing around the herb beds. She held her finger on her lap. The pain had reduced to a dull ache, but she felt like she was in a washing machine, spinning round and round. Black edged the side of her vision. The laughter of the boys seemed to be coming to her down a tunnel. She desperately wanted to lean her head down on to her knees, but the bulge of her stomach was in the way. She propped her elbow on the arm of the chair and leant her head on her arm. If she could just sit still for a few moments, perhaps the feeling would pass.

She became aware that Fi was saying something to her. Other noises returned—the tic tic of the sprinkler, the squeals of the boys, the concerned voices of her friends.

'She's gone very pale,' said Thandie.

'Let me help you inside,' said Fi, 'It's too hot out here.'

Ally felt a hand on her arm helping her out of the chair, leading her through the gate and into a cool building. She sat on a sofa. A glass of cold water was put in her hand. Her head throbbed, her finger throbbed, her stomach kept clenching.

'I'm sure you'll feel better in a moment—' said Thandie.

But she didn't hear the rest. It was all a bit of a blur after that. The girls bundled her into the back of Fi's car. They arrived at hospital. Rob, her husband, appeared beside her bed. He had a white face and pinched lips. She gave his hand a squeeze.

And then the baby, a beautiful baby boy.

'What beautiful blue eyes he has,' squeaked Chloe, sitting on the edge of the bed.

'And such a thick mop of hair,' said Thandie, curling a lock between her fingers.

'Well done,' said Fi.

Ally looked up at the smiling faces of the girls who had come to visit her in hospital.

'You're so brave,' said Chloe, 'I want to be just like you when it's my time.'

Ally looked down at her gorgeous boy, and up at the expectant faces of her friends. 'Maybe not such a wooz after all,' she thought.

Mountain out of a Molehill

Sally Howard

Many cyclists enjoy the rolling downland landscape of the countryside around Winchester. Farley Mount, located four miles west of the city, is hardly a mountain — but is one of the highest points in Hampshire (174 metres).

'It's not that far, Emma. You're making a mountain out of a molehill.'

'Ha ha, Tom. It is a mountain. Look...' Emma jabbed at her phone, her sweaty finger sliding over the home button. She shoved the screen in Tom's face. 'Look, this stretch is 5 km uphill. *Uphill.*'

'It's only Farley Mount,' he said, 'just a gentle—' He broke off when she glared at him. She was gratified that he looked a little nonplussed.

She dropped her bike to the ground with a crunch of metal and sunk down beside it. Sharp stones stuck into her backside, even through her padded cycle shorts. Gravel clattered over the side of the path, raining down into the leafy vegetation on the slope below.

They had cycled all the way from Winchester and were now climbing Farley Mount. The view to her left towards Winchester was fantastic. A rolling patchwork of brown fields and mottled green woods, fading away into the blue green haze of morning. She could even see the glint of the cathedral in the distance.

But it was a steep climb. Tom couldn't deny that. Sun had beaten down on her neck on the way up the twisting path. Sweat tickled down her back. She hated being hot. It made her grumpy. It was very hot. She was very grumpy.

Tom, on the other hand, seemed to have not even broken a sweat. His tanned legs carried him in long effortless strides. She'd kept her eyes on him as he cycled in front. Keep in my slipstream, he'd said. She had tried, for all the help it had given her.

He crouched beside her, retrieving the water bottle from his bike holder and handing it to her. 'Cheer up,' he said. 'It was your idea to come up here after all.'

'Not helpful, Tom. It's easy for you. You're meant to be my coach. Are you going to leave me behind when we do the ride?'

He shrugged. 'We'll head back now,' he said, turning away. He started to fiddle with something on his bike.

She downed a mouthful of warm water from the sports bottle. Droplets ran down her chin. She swiped at them, then ran the back of her wet hand over her burning cheeks. Why had she snapped like that? Her comments were totally uncalled for. Tom hadn't pulled away at all. In fact, he always waited for her. He had been nothing but helpful with her cycle training, coming out with her every Sunday, rain or shine. All she could do was bite out sarcastic remarks.

She heard the crunch of tyres as another Lycra-clad cyclist came up the path. The guy was pushing hard on the pedals. Farley Mount was good training to build hill strength and everyone seemed to be out on this warm spring day. Watching the cyclist power past, once again she regretted entering the cycling challenge that they had both signed up to. The South Downs 100 Sportive. Cycle 100 miles. Including hills. Such madness. What was she thinking?

Tom had mounted his bike. 'C'mon, then,' he said. 'Let's get going before you seize up.' He adjusted his helmet, not looking at her, but surveying the rolling countryside.

She eased herself up. Her calf muscle clenched and she massaged it with her fingers.

Tom, ready on his bike, turned to her. 'Cramp?' he said.

'No, I don't think so. Just a bit sore.'

She got on her bike and pushed off. She followed Tom, falling in behind him, as he led the way back down. She noticed that he was careful not to pull away. She bit her lip and felt thoroughly miserable.

They were on a winding stretch of road when a car tried to pass them on a bend. It didn't pull out far enough. Too late to react, too close to Tom's wheels, a pothole appeared in front of her. A dark, gaping, water-filled hole. Someone ought to fix that, she thought, as her wheel clipped the crumbling edge and she was jerked from her seat.

Her bike skidded into the road, into the path of the car. She heard the clunk of metal on metal. She slid along the ground. A shower of gravel sprayed into her face. Good job I'm wearing sunglasses, she thought. Tom always insisted on that. She ended up in a crumpled heap in the verge.

She felt hands on her back. 'Are you all right?' Tom's voice was full of concern.

Her knee and hip burned. She pulled herself into a sitting position and looked at her leg. It was grazed: long red scratches studded with gravel blossomed across her pale skin. She regretted wearing shorts.

'Are you all right?' Tom sounded even more anxious. His hands dug into her shoulders.

'Yes, I think so.' She nodded. He relaxed his grip.

The driver of the vehicle got out of his car. He was a young lad, with a cap on the wrong way round. Ignoring Emma and the crumpled bike, he bent down to examine the bumper of his car.

Tom stood up, pulling himself to his full height. 'Hey you...'

'Tom, it's all right,' she said. She stood up, leaning on his arm. 'We're insured. It doesn't matter. Just ask him for his details. That's all.'

Tom went over to the driver. Emma limped over to her bike and pulled it from under the wheels of the car. Luckily her phone that she'd attached to the handle bars was okay. The bike was a write-off. She snapped some pictures for evidence, including of the guy and his car, just in case.

The driver got back in his car and drove off. Tom came over. His cheeks were flushed and he ran his hand through his hair. 'Cheeky sod. He said we got in his way!'

Emma touched his arm. 'Let him go.' She pointed to her GoPro, also attached to the front of her bike. 'Hopefully we have it recorded.'

Tom relaxed. 'Of course. Forgot about that.' He looked around, a frown creasing his brow. 'How are we going to get you down from this mountain? I'll have to cycle back and get the car and come and collect you.'

She looked up at him. Sunlight shone on his dark hair. 'Tom, I, um, I didn't mean what I said earlier.'

He nodded. 'It's okay. You're overdoing it, you know.' His face relaxed. 'As your coach I strongly recommend that you listen to me in such matters.'

'Well, coach, I will do that.' Emma grinned back. 'But only in matters pertaining to cycling, just to be clear.' She paused. 'And, did I just hear you admit that this is a mountain after all?'

He shook his head. 'Certainly not. It's *only* Farley Mount. As the more experienced professional here, I can assure you that this is just a gentle climb. Nothing like what we're going to experience on our cycling challenge.' He reached out his hand to her. 'Yep, you haven't seen nothing yet.'

'Ha ha, Tom.'

Twyford Down

Maggie Farran

Twyford Down is an area of chalk downland lying directly to the southeast of Winchester. In 1991 the down was the site of a major protest against a proposed section of the M3 motorway. Thousands took part, hundreds were arrested, and some were jailed.

Imogen tossed her ginger curls and stared at her mother with her piercing green eyes. 'I bet you never did anything wrong when you were young. I bet you were little Miss Perfect.'

Her mother, Clare, stared calmly back at her fifteen year old daughter. She couldn't help but notice that Immie's golden freckles stood out even more when she was angry.

'Don't be ridiculous, Imogen, of course I wasn't perfect. Anyway we're not talking about me. You're grounded for the weekend. I'm not having you bunking off school again to go on a protest march. It's your GCSE year. It's important.'

Imogen shrugged and glared at Clare. 'I can't expect you to understand. I don't think you've ever felt strongly about anything in your life except to nag me about doing my homework or whether I've had enough fruit or vegetables. You've no idea about what's really important. You need to wake up, Mum, before it's too late.'

Imogen slammed the door as she left. The plates on the dresser rattled satisfyingly for her and their nervous little cat dashed out through the cat flap to the peace of the garden.

Clare made herself a cup of tea in her favourite china mug decorated with a picture of Mottisfont roses. She sat down in her sunny kitchen and took a deep breath. She tried to imagine how her life must appear to Imogen.

The kitchen of her Victorian house in Winchester was lovely. It was large and airy with patio doors looking out over the River Itchen and the water meadows. Saint Catherine's Hill stood majestically in the background. Imogen had only ever known this beautiful house and garden. She had grown up going for walks along by the river.

Clare thought back to the early nineties when she had been a student. She had been as fiery and passionate about the environment as Imogen was now about animal rights. As a student Clare had been horrified when she heard that a motorway was to be built through Twyford Down, which would create a hideous scar through the beautiful landscape.

Clare called upstairs to Imogen. 'Come on, Immie, stop sulking and we'll take Arthur for a walk. It's a beautiful day, far too sunny to be hiding away in your room. Anyway, there are a few things I want to tell you about me when I was a student.'

'I couldn't care less about when you were a student and I don't want to go on a walk with my mother,' Imogen bellowed down the stairs.

'I got sent to prison for twenty-eight days.'

Imogen appeared at the kitchen door in a few seconds. 'Did I hear you right, Mum? Are you telling me the truth? Did you really go to prison? What did you do?'

'Well, it's certainly true but you'll have to go on a walk with your little Miss Perfect mother, if you want to find out.'

Clare put a lead on Arthur, their cheeky Border terrier, and crossed the road and joined the path by the river. A stately swan floated past and Arthur barked indignantly.

'Come on, Mum, tell me what happened. How did a goody-goody like you end up in prison and how come you've never told me before?'

'Well, I thought you were too young and I didn't want to give you ideas. I was a student at uni at the time and although you'll find it hard to believe I felt very strongly about things then. You know the motorway that goes along by Saint Catherine's Hill? Well, it wasn't there when I was your age.'

'What's a motorway got to do with going to prison?'

'There was a large group of us who loved Twyford Down and when we heard that a motorway was going to be built through it, we were furious. We didn't want a motorway making a great ugly scar through beautiful countryside. I joined a group of protestors who were camping there. There was a real mixture of people. Some were students like me who just went at the weekends. Others lived there for months at a time. They used to play musical instruments and paint their faces. They even had a goat tethered up there.'

Imogen and Clare sat down on the grass. Clare unclipped Arthur's lead and he toddled around sniffing all the different smells of the river bank.

'I can't imagine you protesting about anything, Mum. You're always so calm.'

'Well, I was different then. I was nineteen and I'd never felt so strongly about anything before. You'd be amazed what we got up to. We used to chain ourselves to the bulldozers to stop the excavations going on.'

'Weren't you scared, Mum? You might have been killed.'

'Of course I was scared. If I'm honest I was terrified. I can't imagine it now, but I felt like a martyr. I was prepared to die for the cause. At least I thought I was. It's all so long ago. I can't imagine that I ever felt so strongly about it all. There was such a sense of community. I suppose we egged each other on. There was one student who even chained himself round the neck to a bulldozer with a bicycle lock. There was a young dad who held his little boy and stood in front of a huge vehicle to prevent it from moving.'

Imogen stared at her mother; her green eyes alight with admiration. 'What was the scariest bit?'

'Oh, I'll never forget that day. It was on the 9th December 1992 and its known now as Yellow Wednesday. A private security firm all dressed in yellow jackets were sent to evict us all from the site. They were just paid thugs with no training at all. One of them dragged me by the hair over flint stones and thorns. He actually pulled out a clump of my hair. It was terrifying. They were deliberately violent and seemed to enjoy hurting us. You know David Bellamy off the television, well he visited the site and said he had never seen anything like it before.'

'Did you go back, Mum?

'Yes, I felt I had to. None of us wanted to give up after all we'd been through.'

'Mum, I can't believe it was you. Tell me about the prison bit.'

'It was July 1993 and five hundred of us marched onto the down. We called it *a requiem for the landscape*. There was a minute's silence for all the destruction that had happened just to build a motorway. All the machinery had gone and there was an enormous ugly gash in the chalk. We all stopped where the new motorway was crossing the floodplain of the river Itchen on a large embankment. Loads of us went for a swim, some naked.'

'Oh gross, Mum. I hope one of them wasn't you.'

'Anyway some of us were arrested for trespass and I had to go to court. The judge was really harsh and we got sentenced to twenty-eight days in prison. I'll never forget what he said about us wearing the martyr's crown and it not being very comfortable.'

'What did Granny say? I bet she was shocked.'

'No, actually she wasn't. She was quite proud of me. You know what Granny is like. She's always been a tough old bird with strong views on everything. I think you're a lot like her, Immie.'

'And you were too, Mum, back then anyway.'

'Yes I was. I've still got it in me, but those twenty-eight days in prison certainly calmed me down a bit.'

Imogen squeezed her mother's hand and looked at her mother with a new admiration. 'I think you were wonderful, Mum. I want to be just like you and Granny.'

Clare smiled back and wondered how long it would be before another argument broke out between her and her wonderful fiery daughter.

About the Authors

Maggie Farran is a retired teacher. She sings in a community choir, is keen on the theatre, and regularly attends plays at Salisbury Playhouse and the Theatre Royal. She enjoys walking by the River Itchen into Winchester, followed by coffee and a cake at the Cathedral Refectory.

After a career as a software engineer, **Catherine Griffin** now writes fantasy novels. She enjoys gardening, walks in the countryside, and browsing Winchester's bookshops and markets.

Sally Howard is a project manager by profession. When she's not writing, she enjoys reading and trying out new recipes in the kitchen. She's a recent convert to cycling—but only when it's sunny!

Afterword

Thanks for reading! We hope you enjoyed our tour of Winchester, past and present. If you did, please take a moment to write a review on Amazon.

The authors would like to dedicate this book to the memory of Barbara Large MBE — friend, mentor, and inspiration to countless writers. Without her, this book would not exist.

Many other people have helped bring these stories to publication. We'd especially like to thank Karen Stephen for her feedback and support.

Several historical stories were inspired by—and researched from—the Hampshire Chronicle and other newspapers, via the British Newspaper Archive.

If you'd like to read more short stories by the same authors, the books *Secret Lives of Chandler's Ford* and *More Secret Lives of Chandler's Ford* can be found on Amazon in both Kindle and paperback formats.

Printed in Great Britain
by Amazon